Goosebumps

TV Special

③

Return of the Mummy

Phantom of the Auditorium

R.L. Stine

Hippo

Scholastic Children's Books,
Commonwealth House, 1–19 New Oxford Street, London WC1A 1NU, UK
a division of Scholastic Ltd
London ~ New York ~ Toronto ~ Sydney ~ Auckland

First published in this edition by Scholastic Ltd, 1997

Return of the Mummy
First published in the USA by Scholastic Inc., 1994
First published in the UK by Scholastic Ltd, 1995
Copyright © Parachute Press, Inc., 1994
Phantom of the Auditorium
First published in the USA by Scholastic Inc., 1994
First published in the UK by Scholastic Ltd, 1996
Copyright © Parachute Press, Inc., 1994

GOOSEBUMPS is a trademark of Parachute Press, Inc.

ISBN: 0 590 19866 1
All rights reserved

Typeset by Contour Typesetters, Southall, London
Printed by Cox & Wyman Ltd, Reading, Berks

10 9 8 7 6 5 4 3

CONTENTS

Return of the Mummy

"Gabe, we will be landing soon," the stewardess told me, leaning over the seat. "Will someone be meeting you at the airport?"

"Yes. Probably an ancient Egyptian pharaoh," I told her. "Or maybe a disgusting, decaying mummy."

She narrowed her eyes at me. "No. Really," she insisted. "Who will be meeting you in Cairo?"

"My uncle Ben," I replied. "But he likes to play practical jokes. Sometimes he dresses in weird costumes and tries to scare me."

"You told me that your uncle was a famous scientist," the stewardess said.

"He is," I replied. "But he's also weird."

She laughed. I liked her a lot. She had pretty blonde hair. And I liked the way she always tilted her head to one side when she talked.

Her name was Nancy, and she had been very nice to me during the long flight to Egypt.

3

She knew it was my first time flying all by myself.

She kept checking on me and asking how I was doing. But she treated me like a grown-up. She didn't bring me one of those stupid join-the-dots books or a plastic wings badge that they always give to kids on planes. And she kept slipping me extra bags of peanuts, even though she wasn't supposed to.

"Why are you visiting your uncle?" Nancy asked. "Just for fun?"

I nodded. "I did it last summer, too," I told her. "It was really awesome! But this year, Uncle Ben has been digging in an unexplored pyramid. He's discovered an ancient, sacred tomb. And he invited me to be with him when he opens it up."

She laughed and tilted her head a little more. "You have a good imagination, Gabe," she said. Then she turned away to answer a man's question.

I *do* have a good imagination. But I wasn't making that up.

My uncle Ben Hassad is a famous archaeologist. He has been digging around in pyramids for lots of years. I've seen newspaper articles about him. And once he was in *National Geographic*.

Last summer, my entire family visited Cairo. My cousin Sari and I—she's Uncle Ben's daughter—had some amazing adventures down

4

in the chambers of the Great Pyramid.

Sari will be there this summer, too, I remembered, staring out of the plane window at the solid blue sky. I wondered if maybe she would give me a break this time.

I like Sari, but she's so competitive! She always has to be the first, the strongest, the smartest, the best. She's the only thirteen-year-old girl I know who can turn eating breakfast into a contest!

"Flight attendants, prepare for landing," the pilot announced over the loudspeaker.

I sat up to get a better view out of the window. As the plane lowered, I could see the city of Cairo beneath us. A slender blue ribbon curled along the city. That, I knew, was the Nile River.

The city stretched out from the river. Peering straight down, I could see tall, glass skyscrapers and low, domed temples. Where the city ended, the desert began. Yellow sand stretched to the horizon.

My stomach began to feel a little fluttery. The pyramids were somewhere out in that desert. And in a day or two, I would be climbing down into one of them, following my uncle into a tomb that hadn't been opened for thousands of years.

What would we find?

I pulled the little mummy hand from my shirt pocket and gazed down at it. It was so tiny—no bigger than a child's hand. I had bought it from a kid at a garage sale for two dollars. He said it was called a "Summoner." He said it could summon ancient evil spirits.

It looked like a mummy hand. The fingers were wrapped in stained gauze bandages, with a little black tar showing through.

I'd thought it was a fake, made of rubber or plastic. I mean, I never thought it was a real mummy hand.

But last summer, the hand had saved all of our lives. The kid who sold it to me was right. It really did bring a bunch of mummies to life! It was *amazing*!

Of course my parents and my friends back home didn't believe my incredible story. And they didn't believe that the Summoner really worked. They said it was just a joke mummy hand made in some souvenir factory. Probably made in Taiwan.

But I carry it with me wherever I go. It is my good luck charm. I'm not very superstitious. I mean, I walk under ladders all the time. And my lucky number is thirteen.

But I really do believe that the little mummy hand will protect me.

The strange thing about the mummy hand is that it is always warm. It doesn't feel like plastic. It feels warm, like a real human hand.

Back home in Michigan, I had a major panic attack when Mum and Dad were packing my suitcase for the flight. I couldn't find the mummy hand. And, of course, there was *no way* I would go to Egypt without it!

I was so relieved when I finally found it. It was tucked into the back pocket of a crumpled-up pair of jeans.

Now, as the plane nosed down for a landing, I reached for the hand in the pocket of my T-shirt. I pulled it out—and gasped.

The hand was cold. Cold as ice!

Why had the mummy hand suddenly turned cold?

Was it some kind of a message? A warning?

Was I heading into danger?

I didn't have time to think about it. The plane rolled into the gate, and the passengers were scrambling to pull down their hand luggage and push their way out of the plane.

I tucked the mummy hand into my jeans pocket, hoisted up my backpack, and headed to the front. I said goodbye to Nancy and thanked her for all the peanuts. Then I followed the others down the long, covered ramp and into the airport.

So many people!

And they all seemed to be in a hurry. They were practically stepping over each other. Men in dark business suits. Women in loose-flowing robes, their faces covered by veils. Teenage girls in jeans and T-shirts. A group of dark, serious-looking men in silky white suits that looked like pyjamas. A family with three little kids, all crying.

I had a sudden sinking feeling. How would I ever find Uncle Ben in this crowd?

My backpack began to feel very heavy. My eyes frantically searched back and forth. Strange voices surrounded me, all talking so loudly. No one was speaking English.

"Ow!" I cried out as I felt a sharp pain in my side.

I turned and realized that a woman had bumped me with her luggage cart.

Stay calm, Gabe, I instructed myself. Just stay calm.

Uncle Ben is here, looking for you. He'll find you. You just have to stay calm.

But what if my uncle forgot? I asked myself. What if he got mixed up about what day I was arriving? Or what if he got busy down in the pyramid and lost track of the time?

I can be a real worrier if I put my mind to it.

And right now I was worrying enough for three people!

If Uncle Ben isn't here, I'll go to a phone and call him, I decided.

For sure.

I could just hear myself saying, "Operator, can I speak to my uncle at the pyramids, please?"

I don't think that would work too well.

I didn't have a phone number for Uncle Ben. I wasn't sure he even *had* a phone out where he was staying. All I knew was that he had been living in a tent somewhere near the pyramid where he was digging.

Gazing frantically around the crowded arrival area, I was just about to give in to total panic— when a large man came walking up to me.

I couldn't see his face. He wore a long, white, hooded robe. It's called a burnoose. And his face was buried inside the hood.

"Taxi?" he asked in a high, shrill voice. "Taxi? American taxi?"

I burst out laughing. "Uncle Ben!" I cried happily.

"Taxi? American taxi? Taxi ride?" he insisted.

"Uncle Ben! I'm so glad to see you!" I exclaimed. I threw my arms around his waist and gave him a big hug. Then, laughing at his stupid disguise, I reached up and pulled back his hood.

The man under the hood had a bald, shaved head and a heavy black moustache. He glared at me furiously.

I had never seen him before in my life.

"Gabe! Gabe! Over here!"

I heard a voice calling my name. Glancing past the angry man, I saw Uncle Ben and Sari. They were waving to me from in front of the reservations counter.

The man's face turned bright red, and he shouted something at me in Arabic. I was glad I couldn't understand him. He kept muttering as he pulled up the hood of his burnoose.

"Sorry about that!" I cried. Then I dodged past him and hurried to greet Uncle Ben and my cousin.

Uncle Ben shook my hand and said, "Welcome to Cairo, Gabe." He was wearing a loose-fitting, white, short-sleeved sportshirt and baggy chinos.

Sari wore faded denim cut-offs and a bright green tank top. She was already laughing at me. A bad start. "Was that a friend of yours?" she teased.

11

"I—I made a mistake," I confessed. I glanced back. The man was still scowling at me.

"Did you really think that was Daddy?" Sari demanded.

I mumbled a reply. Sari and I were the same age. But I saw that she was still an inch taller than me. She had let her black hair grow. It fell down her back in a single plait.

Her big, dark eyes sparkled excitedly. She *loved* making fun of me.

I told them about my flight as we walked to the baggage area to get my suitcase. I told them how Nancy, the stewardess, kept slipping me bags of peanuts.

"I flew here last week," Sari told me. "The stewardess let *me* sit in First Class. Did you know you can have an ice-cream sundae in First Class?"

No, I didn't know that. I could see that Sari hadn't changed a bit.

She goes to a boarding school in Chicago since Uncle Ben has been spending all of his time in Egypt. Of course she gets straight As. And she's a champion skier and tennis player.

Sometimes I feel a little sorry for her. Her mum died when Sari was five. And Sari only gets to see her dad on holidays and during the summer.

But as we waited for my suitcase to come out on the conveyor belt, I wasn't feeling sorry for her at all. She was busy bragging about how this

12

pyramid was twice as big as the one I'd been in last summer. And how she'd already been down in it several times, and how she'd take me on a tour—if I wasn't too afraid.

Finally, my bulging, blue suitcase appeared. I lugged it off the conveyor and dropped it at my feet. It weighed a ton!

I tried to lift it, but I could barely budge it.

Sari pushed me out of the way. "Let *me* get that," she insisted. She grabbed the handle, raised the suitcase off the floor, and started off with it.

"Hey—!" I called after her. What a show-off!

Uncle Ben grinned at me. "I think Sari has been working out," he said. He put a hand on my shoulder and led me towards the glass doors. "Let's get to the jeep."

We loaded the suitcase into the back of the jeep, then headed towards the city. "It's been swelteringly hot during the day," Uncle Ben told me, mopping his broad forehead with a handkerchief. "And then cool at night."

Traffic crawled on the narrow street. Horns honked constantly. Drivers kept their horns going whether they moved or stopped. The noise was deafening.

"We're not stopping in Cairo," Uncle Ben explained. "We're going straight to the pyramid at Al-Jizah. We're all living in tents out there so we can be close to our work."

"I hope you brought insect repellent," Sari complained. "The mosquitoes are as big as frogs!"

"Don't exaggerate," Uncle Ben scolded. "Gabe isn't afraid of a few mosquitoes—are you?"

"No way," I replied quietly.

"How about scorpions?" Sari demanded.

The traffic grew lighter as we left the city behind and headed into the desert. The yellow sand gleamed under the hot afternoon sun. Waves of heat rose up in front of us as the jeep bumped over the narrow, two-lane road.

Before long, a pyramid came into view. Behind the waves of heat off the desert floor, it looked like a wavering mirage. It didn't seem real.

As I stared out at it, my throat tightened with excitement. I had seen the pyramids last summer. But it was still a thrilling sight.

"I can't believe the pyramids are over four thousand years old!" I exclaimed.

"Yeah. That's even older than *me*!" Uncle Ben joked. His expression turned serious. "It fills me with pride every time I see them, Gabe," he admitted. "To think that our ancient ancestors were smart enough and skilled enough to build these marvels."

Uncle Ben was right. I suppose the pyramids have special meaning for me since my family is Egyptian. Both sets of my grandparents came from Egypt. They moved to the United States around 1930. My mum and dad were born in Michigan.

I think of myself as a typical American kid. But there's still something exciting about visiting the country where your ancestors came from.

As we drove nearer, the pyramid appeared to rise up in front of us. Its shadow formed a long, blue triangle over the yellow sand.

Cars and tour buses jammed a small parking lot. I could see a row of saddled camels tethered on one side of the lot. A crowd of tourists stretched across the sand, gazing up at the pyramid, snapping photographs, chatting noisily and pointing.

Uncle Ben turned the jeep on to a narrow side road, and we headed away from the crowd, towards the back of the pyramid. As we drove into the shade, the air suddenly felt cooler.

"I'd *kill* for an ice-cream cone!" Sari wailed. "I've never been so hot in my life!"

"Let's not talk about the heat," Uncle Ben replied, sweat dripping down his forehead into his bushy eyebrows. "Let's talk about how happy you are to see your father after so many months."

Sari groaned. "I'd be happier to see you if you were carrying an ice-cream cone."

Uncle Ben laughed.

A khaki-uniformed guard stepped in front of the jeep. Uncle Ben held up a blue ID card. The guard waved us past.

As we followed the road behind the pyramid, a row of low, white canvas tents came into view. "Welcome to the Pyramid Hilton!" Uncle Ben joked. "That's our luxury suite over there." He pointed to the nearest tent.

"It's pretty comfortable," he said, parking the jeep beside the tent. "But the room service is lousy."

"And you have to watch out for scorpions," Sari warned.

She'd say *anything* to try to scare me.

We unloaded my suitcase. Then Uncle Ben led us up to the base of the pyramid.

A camera crew was packing up its equipment. A young man, covered in dust, climbed out of a low entrance dug into one of the limestone squares. He waved to my uncle, then hurried towards the tents.

"One of my people," Uncle Ben muttered. He motioned towards the pyramid. "Well, here you are, Gabe. A long way from Michigan, huh?"

I nodded. "It's amazing," I told him, shielding my eyes to gaze up to the top. "I'd forgotten how much bigger the pyramids look in person."

16

"Tomorrow I'll take you both down to the tomb," Uncle Ben promised. "You've come at just the right time. We've been digging for months and months. And at long last, we are about to break the seal and enter the tomb itself."

"Wow!" I exclaimed. I wanted to be cool in front of Sari. But I couldn't help it. I was really excited.

"Guess you'll be really famous after you open the tomb, huh, Dad?" Sari asked. She swatted a fly on her arm. "Ow!"

"I'll be so famous, the flies will be afraid to bite you," Uncle Ben replied. "By the way, do you know what they called flies in ancient Egypt?"

Sari and I shook our heads no.

"I don't either!" Uncle Ben said, grinning. One of his stupid jokes. He had an endless supply of them. His expression suddenly changed. "Oh. That reminds me. I have a present for you, Gabe."

"A present?"

"Now, where did I put it?" He dug both hands into the pockets of his baggy chinos.

As he searched, I saw something move behind him. A shadow over my uncle's shoulder, back at the low opening to the pyramid.

I squinted at it.

The shadow moved. A figure stepped out slowly.

17

At first I thought the sun was playing tricks on my eyes.

But as I squinted harder, I realized that I was seeing correctly.

The figure stepped out from the pyramid—its face was covered in worn, yellowed gauze. So were its arms. And its legs.

I opened my mouth to cry out—but my voice choked in my throat.

And as I struggled to alert my uncle, the mummy stiffly stretched out its arms and came staggering up behind him.

I saw Sari's eyes grow wide with fright. She let out a low gasp.

"Uncle Ben—!" I finally managed to scream. "Turn around! It—it—!"

My uncle narrowed his eyes at me, confused.

The mummy staggered closer, its hands reaching out menacingly, about to grab the back of Uncle Ben's neck.

"A *mummy*!" I shrieked.

Uncle Ben spun around. He let out a startled cry. "It walks!" he shouted, pointing at the mummy with a trembling finger. He backed away as the mummy advanced. "It walks!"

"Ohhh." A strange moan escaped Sari's lips.

I turned and started to run.

But then the mummy burst out laughing.

It lowered its yellowed arms. "Boo!" it cried, and laughed again.

I turned and saw that Uncle Ben was laughing, too. His dark eyes sparkled gleefully. "It walks! It walks!" he repeated, shaking his head. He put his arm around the mummy's shoulder.

I gaped at the two of them, my heart still pounding.

"This is John," Uncle Ben said, enjoying the joke he'd pulled on us. "He's been doing a TV advert here. For some new kind of stickier bandage."

"Sticky Bird Bandages," John told us. "They're just what your mummy ordered!"

He and Uncle Ben enjoyed another good laugh at that. Then my uncle pointed to the camera crew, packing their equipment into a small van. "They've finished for the day. But John agreed to hang around and help me scare you."

Sari rolled her eyes. "Nice try," she said dryly. "You'll have to do better than that, Daddy, to frighten me." And then she added, "Poor Gabe. Did you see his face? He was so freaked out! I thought he was going to spontaneously *combust* or something!"

Uncle Ben and John laughed.

"Hey—no way!" I insisted, feeling my face turn red.

How could Sari *say* that? When the mummy staggered out, I saw her gasp and back away. She was just as scared as I was!

"I heard you scream, too!" I told her. I didn't mean to sound so whiny.

"I just did that to help them scare you," Sari

insisted. She tossed her long plait over her shoulder.

"I've got to run," John said, glancing at his wristwatch. "As soon as we get back to the hotel, I'm going to hit the pool. I may stay underwater for a week!" He gave us a wave of his bandaged hand and went jogging to the van.

Why hadn't I noticed that he was wearing a wristwatch?

I felt like a total dork. "That's it!" I cried angrily to my uncle. "I'm never falling for one of your stupid jokes again! Never!"

He grinned at me and winked. "Want to bet?"

"What about Gabe's present?" Sari asked. "What is it?"

Uncle Ben pulled something out of his pocket and held it up. A pendant on a string. Made of clear orange glass. It gleamed in the bright sunlight.

He handed it to me. I moved it in my hand, feeling its smoothness as I examined it. "What is it?" I asked him. "What kind of glass is this?"

"It isn't glass," he replied. "It's a clear stone called amber." He stepped closer to examine it along with me. "Hold it up and look inside the pendant."

I followed his instructions. I saw a large brown bug inside. "It looks like some kind of beetle," I said.

"It *is* a beetle," Uncle Ben said, squinting one

eye to see it better. "It's an ancient beetle called a *scarab*. It was trapped in the amber four thousand years ago. As you can see, it's perfectly preserved."

"That's really gross," Sari commented, making a face. She slapped Uncle Ben on the back. "Great gift, Dad. A dead bug. Remind me not to let you do our Christmas shopping!"

Uncle Ben laughed. Then he turned back to me. "The scarab was very important to the ancient Egyptians," he said, rolling the amber pendant in his fingers, then dropping it back into my palm. "They believed that scarabs were a symbol of immortality."

I stared at the bug's dark shell, its six prickly legs, perfectly preserved.

"To keep a scarab meant immortality," my uncle continued. "But the bite of a scarab meant instant death."

"Weird," Sari muttered.

"It's great-looking," I told him. "Is it really four thousand years old?"

He nodded. "Wear it around your neck, Gabe. Maybe it still has some of its ancient powers."

I slipped the pendant over my head and adjusted it under my T-shirt. The amber stone felt cool against my skin. "Thanks, Uncle Ben," I said. "It's a great present."

He mopped his sweaty forehead with a wadded-up handkerchief. "Let's go back to the tent and get something cold to drink," he said.

We took a few steps—and then stopped when we saw Sari's face.

Her entire body trembled. Her mouth dropped open as she pointed to my chest.

"Sari—what *is* it?" Uncle Ben cried.

"The s-scarab—" she stammered. "It . . . escaped! I saw it!" She pointed down. "It's there!"

"Huh?" I spun away from her and bent down to find the scarab.

"Ow!" I cried out when I felt a sharp stab of pain on the back of my leg.

And realized the scarab had bitten me.

As I gasped in alarm, Uncle Ben's words about the scarab rushed through my mind.

"To keep a scarab meant immortality. But the bite of a scarab meant instant death."

Instant death?

"Noooo!" I let out a howl and spun around.

And saw Sari hunched down on her knees. Grinning. Her hand outstretched.

And realized she had pinched my leg.

My heart still pounding, I grabbed the pendant and stared into the orange glassy stone. The scarab was still frozen inside, just as it had been for four thousand years.

"Aaaaaaaggh!" I let out a howl of rage. I was mostly furious at myself.

Was I going to fall for every stupid joke Uncle Ben and Sari played on me this trip? If so, it was going to be a very long summer.

I had always liked my cousin. Except for the times when she was being so competitive

24

and so superior, we always got along really well.

But now I wanted to punch her. I wanted to say really nasty things to her.

But I couldn't think of anything nasty enough.

"That was really mean, Sari," I said glumly, tucking the pendant under my T-shirt.

"Yes, it was—*wasn't* it!" she replied, very pleased with herself.

That night, I lay on my back on my narrow camp bed, staring up at the low tent roof, listening. Listening to the brush of the wind against the tent door, the soft creak of the tent poles, the flap of the canvas.

I don't think I'd ever felt so alert.

Turning my head, I could see the pale glow of moonlight through a crack in the tent door. I could see blades of dried desert grass on the sand outside. I could see water stains on the tent wall over my bed.

I'll never get to sleep, I thought unhappily.

I pushed and punched the flat pillow for the twentieth time, trying to fluff it up. The harsh wool blanket felt scratchy against my chin.

I'd slept away from home before. But I'd always slept in a room of some kind. Not in the middle of a vast, sandy desert in a tiny, flapping, creaking, canvas tent.

I wasn't scared. My uncle lay snoring away in his bed a few feet across the tent.

I was just alert. Very, very alert.

So alert I could hear the swish of palm trees outside. And I could hear the low hum of car tyres miles away on the narrow road.

And I heard the thudding of my heart when something wriggled on my chest.

I was so alert. I felt it instantly.

Just a tickle. A quick, light move.

It could only be one thing. The scarab moving inside the amber pendant.

No joke this time.

No joke. It moved.

I fumbled for the pendant in the dark, tossing down the blanket. I held it up to the moonlight. I could see the fat beetle in there, black in its orange prison.

"Did you move?" I whispered to it. "Did you wriggle your legs?"

I suddenly felt really stupid. Why was I whispering to a four-thousand-year-old insect? Why was I imagining that it was alive?

Annoyed with myself, I tucked the pendant back under my nightshirt.

I had no way of knowing how important that pendant would soon become to me.

I had no way of knowing that the pendant held a secret that would either save my life. Or kill me.

The tent was already hot when I awoke the next morning. Bright yellow sunlight poured in through the open tent flap. Squinting against the light, I rubbed my eyes and stretched. Uncle Ben had already gone out.

My back ached. The camp bed was so hard!

But I was too excited to worry about my back. I was going down into the pyramid this morning to the entrance of an ancient tomb.

I pulled on a clean T-shirt and the jeans I'd worn the day before. I adjusted the scarab pendant under the T-shirt. Then I carefully tucked the little mummy hand into the back pocket of my jeans.

With the pendant and the mummy hand, I'm well protected, I told myself. Nothing bad can happen on this trip.

I pulled a hairbrush through my thick, black hair a few times, and tugged my black-and-yellow Michigan Wolverines cap on. Then I hurried to the mess tent to get some breakfast.

The sun was floating above the palm trees in the distance. The yellow desert sand gleamed brightly. I took a deep breath of fresh air.

Yuck. There must be some camels nearby, I decided. The air wasn't exactly fresh.

I found Sari and Uncle Ben having their breakfast, seated at the end of the long table in the mess tent. Uncle Ben wore his usual baggy chinos and a short-sleeved, white sportshirt with coffee stains down the front.

Sari had her long, black hair pulled straight back in a ponytail. She wore a bright red tank top over white tennis shorts.

They greeted me as I entered the tent. I poured myself a glass of orange juice and, since I didn't see any Frosted Flakes, filled a bowl with raisin bran.

Three of Uncle Ben's workers were eating at the other end of the table. They were talking excitedly about their work. "We could go in today," I heard one of them say.

"It might take days to break the seal on the tomb door," a young woman replied.

I sat down next to Sari. "Tell me all about the tomb," I said to Uncle Ben. "Whose tomb is it? What's in there?"

He chuckled. "Let me say good morning before I launch into a lecture."

29

Sari leaned over my cereal bowl. "Hey, look—" she said, pointing. "I got a lot more raisins than you did!"

I *told* you she could turn breakfast into a contest.

"Well, I got more pulp in my orange juice," I replied.

It was just a joke, but she checked her juice glass to make sure.

Uncle Ben wiped his mouth with a paper napkin. He took a long sip of black coffee. "If I'm not mistaken," he began, "the tomb we have discovered here belonged to a prince. Actually, a cousin of King Tutankhamen."

"That's King Tut," Sari told me, interrupting.

"I know that!" I replied sharply.

"King Tut's tomb was discovered in 1922," Uncle Ben continued. "The vast burial chamber was filled with most of Tut's treasures. It was the most amazing archaeological discovery of the century." A smile crossed his face. "Until now."

"Do you think you've found something even more amazing?" I asked. I hadn't touched my cereal. I was too interested in my uncle's story.

He shrugged. "There's no way of knowing what's behind the tomb door until we open it, Gabe. But I have my fingers crossed. I believe we've found the burial chamber of Prince

30

Khor-Ru. He was the king's cousin. And he was said to be as wealthy as the king."

"And do you think all of Prince Khor-Ru's crowns, and jewels and belongings are buried with him?" Sari asked.

Uncle Ben took the last sip of coffee and slid the white mug across the table. "Who knows?" he replied. "There could be amazing treasures in there. Or it could be empty. Just an empty room."

"How could it be empty?" I demanded. "Why would there be an empty tomb in the pyramids?"

"Grave robbers," Uncle Ben replied, frowning. "Remember, Prince Khor-Ru was buried sometime around 1300 BC. Over the centuries, thieves broke into the pyramids and robbed the treasures from many burial chambers."

He stood up and sighed. "We may have been digging for all these months only to find an empty room."

"No way!" I cried excitedly. "I bet we will find the Prince's mummy in there. And millions of pounds' worth of jewels!"

Uncle Ben smiled at me. "Enough talk," he said. "Finish your breakfast so we can go and find out."

Sari and I followed Uncle Ben out of the tent. He waved to two young men who came out of the supply tent carrying digging equipment. Then he hurried over to talk to them.

Sari and I lingered back. She turned to me, a serious expression on her face. "Hey, Gabe," she said softly, "sorry I've been such a pain."

"You? A pain?" I replied sarcastically.

She didn't laugh. "I'm a bit worried," she confessed. "About Daddy."

I glanced at Uncle Ben. He was slapping one of the young men on the back as he talked. His usual jolly self.

"Why are you worried?" I asked Sari. "Your dad is in a great mood."

"That's why I'm worried," Sari whispered. "He's so happy and excited. He really thinks this is going to be the discovery that makes him famous."

"So?" I demanded.

"So what if it turns out to be an empty room?" Sari replied, her dark eyes watching her father. "What if grave robbers did strip the place? Or what if it isn't that prince's tomb after all? What if Daddy breaks the seal, opens the door—and finds nothing but a dusty old room filled with snakes?"

She sighed. "Daddy will be heartbroken. Just heartbroken. He's counting on this so much, Gabe. I don't know if he'll be able to take the disappointment."

"Why look on the gloomy side?" I replied. "What if—"

I stopped because Uncle Ben was hurrying back to us. "Let's go down to the chamber," he said excitedly. "The workers think we are very close to uncovering the tomb entrance."

He put an arm on each of our shoulders and guided us to the pyramid.

As we stepped into the shade of the pyramid, the air grew cooler. The low entrance dug at the bottom of the back wall came into view. It was just big enough for us to enter one at a time. Peering into the narrow hole, I saw that the tunnel dropped steeply.

I hope I don't fall, I thought, a heavy knot of fear tightening my stomach. I pictured myself falling and falling down an endless, dark hole.

Mainly, I didn't want to fall in front of Sari. I knew she'd never let me forget it.

Uncle Ben handed Sari and me bright yellow hard hats. They had lights built into them, like miners' hats. "Stick close together," he instructed. "I remember last summer. You two wandered off and got us into a lot of trouble."

"W-we will," I stammered. I was trying not to sound nervous, but I couldn't help it.

I glanced at Sari. She was adjusting the yellow hard hat over her hair. She seemed as calm and confident as ever.

"I'll lead the way," Uncle Ben said, pulling the chin strap under his chin. He turned and started to lower himself into the hole.

But a shrill cry from behind us made us all stop and turn around.

"Stop! Please—stop! Don't go in!"

A young woman came running across the sand.
Her long, black hair flew behind her head as she
ran. She carried a brown briefcase in one hand.
A camera, strapped around her neck, bobbed in
front of her.

She stopped in front of us and smiled at Uncle
Ben. "Dr Hassad?" she asked breathlessly.

My uncle nodded. "Yes?" He waited for her to
catch her breath.

Wow. She's really pretty, I thought. She had
long, black hair, sleek and shiny. She had a
fringe cut straight across her forehead. Beneath
the fringe were the most beautiful green eyes I'd
ever seen.

She was dressed all in white. A white suit
jacket and a white blouse over white slacks.
She was short—only an inch or two taller than
Sari.

She must be a movie star or something, I told
myself. She's so great-looking!

She set her briefcase down on the sand and brushed back her long, black hair. "I'm sorry I shouted like that, Dr Hassad," she told my uncle. "It's just that I needed to talk to you. I didn't want you to disappear into the pyramid."

Uncle Ben narrowed his eyes at her, studying her. "How did you get past the security guard?" he asked, pulling off the hard hat.

"I showed them my press card," she replied. "I'm a reporter for the Cairo *Sun*. My name is Nila Rahmad. I was hoping—"

"Nila?" Uncle Ben interrupted. "What a pretty name."

She smiled. "Yes. My mother named me after the River of Life, the Nile."

"Well, it's a very pretty name," Uncle Ben replied. His eyes twinkled. "But I'm not ready to have any reporters write about our work here."

Nila frowned and bit her lower lip. "I spoke to Dr Fielding a few days ago," she said.

My uncle's eyes widened in surprise. "You did?"

"Dr Fielding gave me permission to write about your discovery," Nila insisted, her green eyes locked on my uncle.

"Well, we haven't discovered anything yet!" Uncle Ben said sharply. "There may not be anything to discover."

"That's not what Dr Fielding told me," Nila replied. "He seemed confident that you were

36

about to make a discovery that would shock the world."

Uncle Ben laughed. "Sometimes my partner gets excited and talks too much," he told Nila.

Nila's eyes pleaded with my uncle. "May I come into the pyramid with you?" She glanced at Sari and me. "I see you have two other visitors."

"My daughter, Sari, and my nephew, Gabe," Uncle Ben replied.

"Well, could I come down with them?" Nila pleaded. "I promise I won't write a word for my paper until you give me permission."

Uncle Ben rubbed his chin thoughtfully. He swung the hard hat back on to his head. "No photographs, either," he muttered.

"Does that mean I can come?" Nila asked excitedly.

Uncle Ben nodded. "As an observer." He was trying to act real tough. But I could see he liked her.

Nila flashed him a warm smile. "Thank you, Dr Hassad."

He reached into the storage cart and handed her a yellow hard hat. "We won't be making any amazing discoveries today," he warned her. "But we're getting very close—to something."

As she slipped on the heavy helmet, Nila turned to Sari and me. "Is this your first time in the pyramid?" she asked.

"No way. I've already been down three times," Sari boasted. "It's really awesome."

"I just arrived yesterday," I said. "So it's my first time down in—"

I stopped when I saw Nila's expression change.

Why was she staring at me like that?

I glanced down and realized that she was staring at the amber pendant. Her mouth was open in shock.

"No! I don't believe this! I really don't! This is so *weird*!" she exclaimed.

"Wh-what's wrong?" I stammered.

"We're *twins!*" Nila declared. She reached under her suit jacket and pulled out a pendant she wore around her neck.

An amber pendant, shaped exactly like mine.

"How unusual!" Uncle Ben exclaimed.

Nila grasped my pendant between her fingers and lowered her face to examine it. "You have a scarab inside yours," she told me, turning the pendant around in her fingers.

She dropped mine and held hers up for me to see. "Look, Gabe. Mine is empty."

I gazed into her pendant. It looked like clear orange glass. Nothing inside.

"I think *yours* is prettier," Sari told Nila. "I wouldn't want to wear a dead bug around my neck."

"But it's supposed to be good luck or something," Nila replied. She tucked the pendant back under her white jacket. "I hope it isn't *bad* luck to have an empty one!"

"I hope so, too," Uncle Ben commented dryly. He turned and led us into the pyramid opening.

I'm not really sure how I got lost.

Sari and I were walking together behind Uncle Ben and Nila. We were close behind them. I could hear my uncle explaining about how the tunnel walls were granite and limestone.

Our helmet lights were on. The narrow beams of yellow light darted and crisscrossed over the dusty tunnel floor and walls as we made our way deeper and deeper into the pyramid.

The ceiling hung low, and we all had to stoop as we walked. The tunnel kept curving, and there were several smaller tunnels that branched off. "False starts and dead ends," Uncle Ben called them.

It was hard to see in the flickering light from our helmets. I stumbled once and scraped my elbow against the rough tunnel wall. It was surprisingly cool down here, and I wished I had worn a sweatshirt or something.

Up ahead, Uncle Ben was telling Nila about King Tut and Prince Khor-Ru. It sounded to me as if Uncle Ben was trying to impress her. I wondered if he had a crush on her or something.

"This is so thrilling!" I heard Nila exclaim. "It was so nice of Dr Fielding and you to let me see it."

"Who is Dr Fielding?" I whispered to Sari.

"My father's partner," Sari whispered back. "But Daddy doesn't like him. You'll probably meet him. He's always around. I don't like him much, either."

I stopped to examine a strange-looking marking on the tunnel wall. It was shaped like some kind of animal head. "Sari—look!" I whispered. "An ancient drawing."

Sari rolled her eyes. "It's Bart Simpson," she muttered. "One of Daddy's workers must have drawn it there."

"I knew that!" I lied. "I was just teasing you."

When I was going to stop making a fool of myself in front of my cousin?

I turned back from the stupid drawing on the wall—and Sari had vanished.

I could see the narrow beam of light from her hard hat up ahead. "Hey—wait up!" I called. But the light disappeared as the tunnel curved away.

And then I stumbled again.

My helmet hit the tunnel wall. And the light went out.

"Hey—Sari? Uncle Ben?" I called to them. I leaned heavily against the wall, afraid to move in the total darkness.

"Hey—! Can anybody hear me?" My voice echoed down the narrow tunnel.

But no one replied.

I pulled off the hard hat and fiddled with the

41

light. I turned it, trying to tighten it. Then I shook the whole hat. But the light wouldn't come back on.

Sighing, I strapped the hat back on to my head.

Now what? I thought, starting to feel a little afraid. My stomach began fluttering. My throat suddenly felt dry.

"Hey—can anybody hear me?" I shouted. "I'm in the dark back here. I can't see!"

No reply.

Where *were* they? Didn't they notice that I had disappeared?

"Well, I'll just wait right here for them," I murmured to myself.

I leaned my shoulder against the tunnel wall—and fell right through the wall.

No way to catch my balance. Nothing to grab on to.

I was falling, falling down through total darkness.

My hands flailed wildly as I fell.

I reached out frantically for something to grab on to.

It all happened too fast to cry out.

I landed hard on my back. Pain shot out through my arms and legs. The darkness swirled around me.

My breath was knocked right out of me. I saw bright flashes of red, then everything went black again. I struggled to breathe, but couldn't suck in any air.

I had that horrible heavy feeling in my chest, like when a basketball hits you in the stomach.

Finally, I sat up, struggling to see in the total darkness. I heard a soft, shuffling sound. Something scraping over the hard dirt floor.

"Hey—can anyone hear me?" My voice came out a hoarse whisper.

Now my back ached, but I was starting to breathe normally.

"Hey—I'm down here!" I called, a little louder. No reply.

Didn't they miss me? Weren't they looking for me?

I was leaning back on my hands, starting to feel better. My right hand started to itch.

I reached to scratch it and brushed something away.

And realized my legs were itching, too. And felt something crawling on my left wrist.

I shook my hand hard. "What's going on here?" I whispered to myself.

My entire body tingled. I felt soft pinpricks up my arms and legs.

Shaking both arms, I jumped to my feet. And banged my helmet against a low ledge.

The light flickered on.

I gasped when I saw the crawling creatures in the narrow beam of light.

Spiders. Hundreds of bulby, white spiders, thick on the chamber floor.

They scuttled across the floor, climbing over each other. As I jerked my head up and the light swept up with it, I saw that the stone walls were covered with them, too. The white spiders made the wall appear to move, as if it were alive.

Spiders hung on invisible threads from the chamber ceiling. They seemed to bob and float in mid-air.

I shook one off the back of my hand.

And, with a gasp, realized why my legs itched. Spiders were crawling all over them. Up over my arms. Down my back.

"Help—somebody! Please!" I managed to cry out.

I felt a spider drop on to the top of my head.

I brushed it away with a frantic slap. "Somebody—help me!" I screamed. "Can anyone hear me?"

And then I saw something scarier. Much scarier. A snake slid down from above me, lowering itself rapidly towards my face.

I ducked and tried to cover my head as the snake silently dropped towards me.

"Grab it!" I heard someone call. "Grab on to it!"

With a startled cry, I raised my eyes. The light beam followed. And I saw that it was not a snake that stretched from above—but a rope.

"Grab on to it, Gabe! Hurry!" Sari shouted urgently from high above.

Brushing away spiders, kicking frantically to shake them off my trainers, I grasped the rope with both hands.

And felt myself being tugged up, pulled up through the darkness to the tunnel floor above.

A few seconds later, Uncle Ben reached down and grabbed me under the shoulders. As he hoisted me up, I could see Sari and Nila pulling with all their might on the rope.

I cheered happily as my feet touched solid ground. But I didn't have long to celebrate. My

46

entire body felt as if it were on fire!

I went wild, kicking my legs, brushing spiders off my arms, scratching spiders off my back, stamping on the spiders as they scuttled off me.

Glancing up, I saw that Sari was laughing at me. "Gabe, what do you call that dance?" she asked.

Uncle Ben and Nila laughed, too. "How did you fall down there, Gabe?" my uncle demanded, peering down into the spider chamber.

"The wall—it gave way," I told him, frantically scratching my legs.

"I thought you were still with me," Sari explained. "When I turned around . . ." Her voice trailed off.

The light on Uncle Ben's helmet beamed down to the lower chamber. "That's a long fall," Uncle Ben said, turning back to me. "Are you sure you're okay?"

I nodded. "Yeah. I think so. It knocked the wind out of me. And then the spiders—"

"There must be hundreds of chambers like that," my uncle commented, glancing at Nila. "The pyramid builders made a maze of tunnels and chambers—to fool tomb robbers and keep them from finding the real tomb."

"Yuck! Such fat spiders!" Sari groaned, stepping back.

"There are millions of them down there," I told

47

her. "On the walls, hanging from the ceiling—everywhere."

"This is going to give me bad dreams," Nila said softly, moving closer to Uncle Ben.

"You sure you're okay?" my uncle demanded again.

I started to reply. Then I suddenly remembered something. The mummy hand. It was tucked in my back pocket.

Had it been crushed when I landed on it?

My heart skipped a beat. I didn't want anything bad to happen to that little hand. It was my good luck charm.

I reached into my jeans pocket and pulled it out. Holding it under the light from my hard hat, I examined it carefully.

I breathed a sigh of relief when I saw that it was okay. It still felt cold. But it hadn't been crushed.

"What's that?" Nila asked, leaning closer to see it better. She brushed her long hair away from her face. "Is that The Summoner?"

"How did you know that?" I demanded, holding the hand up so she could see it better.

Nila stared at it intently. "I know a lot about ancient Egypt," she replied. "I've studied it my whole life."

"It might be an ancient relic," Uncle Ben broke in.

48

"Or it might just be a tacky souvenir," Sari added.

"It has real powers," I insisted, brushing it off carefully. "I landed on it down there—" I pointed to the spider chamber—"and it didn't get crushed."

"I guess it *is* a good luck charm," Nila said, turning back to Uncle Ben.

"Then why didn't it keep Gabe from falling through that wall?" Sari cracked.

Before I could answer, I saw the mummy hand move. The tiny fingers slowly curled. Out and then in.

I cried out and nearly dropped it.

"Gabe—now what?" Uncle Ben demanded sharply.

"Uh . . . nothing," I replied.

They wouldn't believe me anyway.

"I think we've done enough exploring for now," Uncle Ben said.

As we made our way to the entrance, I held the mummy hand in front of me.

I wasn't seeing things. I knew that for sure. The fingers really had moved.

But why?

Was the hand trying to signal to me? Was it trying to warn me about something?

Two days later, Uncle Ben's workers reached the doorway to the burial chamber.

Sari and I had spent the two days hanging around in the tent or exploring the area outside the pyramid. Since it was mostly sand, there wasn't much to explore.

We spent one long afternoon playing game after game of Scrabble. Playing Scrabble with Sari wasn't much fun at all. She is a very defensive player and spent hours figuring out ways to clog the board and block me from getting any good words.

Whenever I put down a really good word, Sari claimed it wasn't a real word and couldn't be allowed. And since we didn't have a dictionary in the tent, she won most of the arguments.

Uncle Ben, meanwhile, seemed really stressed out. I thought maybe he was nervous about finally opening the tomb.

He barely spoke to Sari and me. Instead, he

spent a lot of time meeting with people I didn't recognize. He seemed very serious and business-like. None of his usual backslapping and joking.

Uncle Ben also spent a lot of time talking to Nila. At first, she'd said she wanted to write about his discovery in the pyramid. But now she'd decided to write an article about him. She wrote down nearly every word he said in a little pad she carried with her.

Then, at breakfast, he finally smiled for the first time in two days. "Today's the day," he announced.

Sari and I couldn't hide our excitement. "Are you taking us with you?" I asked.

Uncle Ben nodded. "I want you to be there," he replied. "Perhaps we will make history today. Perhaps it will be a day you will want to remember for the rest of your lives." He shrugged and added thoughtfully: "Perhaps."

A few minutes later, the three of us followed several workers across the sand towards the pyramid. It was a grey day. Heavy clouds hovered low in the sky, threatening rain. The pyramid rose up darkly to meet the clouds.

As we approached the small opening in the back wall, Nila came running up, her camera bobbing in front of her. She wore a long-sleeved, blue denim work shirt over loose-fitting, faded jeans. Uncle Ben greeted her warmly. "But still no photographs," he told her firmly. "Promise?"

Nila smiled back at him. Her green eyes lit up excitedly. She raised a hand to her heart. "Promise."

We all took yellow hard hats from the equipment dump. Uncle Ben was carrying a large stone mallet. He lowered himself into the entrance, and we followed.

My heart was racing as I hurried to keep up with Sari. The lights from our helmets darted over the narrow tunnel. Far up ahead, I could hear the voices of workers and the steady scrape of their digging tools.

"This is really awesome!" I exclaimed breathlessly to Sari.

"Maybe the tomb is filled with jewels," Sari whispered as we made our way around a curve. "Sapphires and rubies and emeralds. Maybe I'll get to try on a jewelled crown worn by an Egyptian princess."

"Do you think there's a mummy in the tomb?" I asked. I wasn't too interested in jewels. "Do you think the mummified body of Prince Khor-Ru is lying there, waiting to be discovered?"

Sari made a disgusted face. "Is that all you can think about—mummies?"

"Well, we *are* in an ancient Egyptian pyramid!" I shot back.

"There could be millions of pounds' worth of jewels and relics in that tomb," Sari scolded.

"And all you can think about is some mouldy old body wrapped up in tar and gauze." She shook her head. "You know, most kids get over their fascination with mummies by the time they're eight or nine."

"Uncle Ben didn't!" I replied.

That shut her up.

We followed Nila and Uncle Ben in silence. After a while, the narrow tunnel curved up sharply. The air grew warmer as we followed it up.

I could see lights ahead. Two battery-powered spotlights were trained on the far wall. As we drew closer, I realized it wasn't a wall. It was a door.

Four workers—two men and two women— were on their knees, working with small shovels and picks. They were scraping the last chunks of dirt away from the door.

"It looks beautiful!" Uncle Ben cried, running up to the workers. They turned to greet him. "It's awesome in the true sense of the word!" he declared.

Nila, Sari, and I stepped up behind him. Uncle Ben was right. The ancient door really was awesome!

It wasn't very tall. I could see that Uncle Ben would have to stoop to step into it. But it looked like a door fit for a prince.

The dark mahogany wood—now petrified—

53

must have been brought from far away. I knew that kind of wood didn't come from any trees that grew in Egypt.

Strange hieroglyphics covered the door from top to bottom. I recognized birds, and cats, and other animals etched deeply into the dark wood.

The most startling sight of all was the seal that locked the door—a snarling lion's head, sculpted in gold. The light from the spotlights made the lion glow like the sun.

"The gold is soft," I heard one of the workers tell my uncle. "The seal will break away easily."

Uncle Ben lowered his heavy mallet to the ground. He stared for a long moment at the glowing lion's head, then turned back to us. "They thought this lion would scare any intruders away from the tomb," he explained. "I guess it worked. Till now."

"Dr Hassad, I have to photograph the actual breaking of the seal," Nila said, stepping up beside him. "You really must let me. We can't let the moment go unrecorded."

He gazed at her thoughtfully. "Well ... okay," he agreed.

A pleased smile crossed her face as she raised her camera. "Thanks, Ben."

The workers stepped back. One of them handed Uncle Ben a hammer and a delicate tool that looked like a doctor's scalpel. "It's all yours, Dr Hassad," she said.

Uncle Ben raised the tools and stepped up to the seal. "Once I break this seal, we will open the door and step into a room that hasn't been seen in four thousand years," he announced.

Nila steadied her camera over her eye, carefully adjusting the lens.

Sari and I moved up beside the workers.

The gold lion appeared to glow brighter as Uncle Ben raised the tool. A hush fell over the tunnel. I could feel the excitement, feel the tension in the air.

Such suspense!

I realized I had been holding my breath. I let it out in a long, silent whoosh and took another.

I glanced at Sari. She was nervously chewing her lower lip. Her hands were pressed tightly at her sides.

"Anyone hungry? Maybe we should forget about this and send out for a pizza!" Uncle Ben joked.

We all laughed loudly.

That was Uncle Ben for you—cracking a dumb joke at what might be the most exciting moment of his life.

The tense silence returned. Uncle Ben's expression turned serious. He turned back to the ancient seal. He raised the small chisel to the back of the seal. Then he started to lift the hammer.

And a booming voice rang out, "PLEASE—LET ME REST IN PEACE!"

I let out a startled cry.

"LET ME REST IN PEACE!" the booming voice repeated.

I saw Uncle Ben lower his chisel. He spun around, his eyes wide with surprise.

I realized the voice came from behind us. I turned to see a man I had never seen before, half hidden in the shadowy tunnel. He made his way towards us, taking long, steady strides.

He was a tall, lanky man, so tall he really had to hunch his shoulders in the low tunnel. Bald except for a fringe of dark hair at the ears, he had a slender face, an unfriendly scowl on his thin lips.

He wore a perfectly ironed safari jacket over a shirt and tie. His black eyes, like little raisins, glared at my uncle. I wondered if the man ever ate. He was as skinny as a mummy himself!

"Omar—!" Uncle Ben started. "I wasn't expecting you back from Cairo."

"Let me rest in peace," Dr Fielding repeated, softer this time. "Those are the words of Prince Khor-Ru. Written on the ancient stone we found last month. That was the prince's wish."

"Omar, we've been over this before," my uncle replied, sighing. He lowered the hammer and chisel to his sides.

Dr Fielding pushed past Sari and me as if we weren't there. He stopped in front of my uncle and swept a hand back over his bald head.

"Well, then, how can you dare to break the seal?" Dr Fielding demanded.

"I am a scientist," my uncle replied slowly, speaking each word clearly and distinctly. "I cannot allow superstition to stand in the way of discovery, Omar."

"I am also a scientist," Dr Fielding replied, using both hands to tighten his tie. "But I am not willing to defile this ancient tomb. I am not willing to go against the wishes of Prince Khor-Ru. And I am not willing to call the words of the hieroglyph mere superstition."

"This is where we disagree," Uncle Ben said softly. He motioned to the four workers. "We have spent too many months, too many years, to stop just outside the door. We have come this far, Omar. We must go the rest of the way."

Dr Fielding chewed his lower lip. He pointed to the top of the door. "Look, Ben. There are the same hieroglyphs as on the stone. The same warning. *Let me rest in peace.*"

"I know, I know," my uncle said, frowning.

"The warning is very clear," Dr Fielding continued heatedly, his tiny raisin eyes narrowed at my uncle. "If anyone should disturb the prince, if anyone should repeat the ancient words written on the tomb five times—the mummified prince shall come to life. And he shall seek his vengeance on those who disturbed him."

Listening to those words made me shudder. I stared hard at Uncle Ben. Why hadn't he ever told Sari and me about the prince's threat? Why hadn't he ever mentioned the words of warning they had found on an ancient stone?

Was he afraid he might frighten us?

Was he frightened himself?

No. No way.

He didn't seem at all frightened now as he argued with Dr Fielding. I could tell they had had this argument before. And I could see there was no way that Dr Fielding was going to stop my uncle from breaking the seal and entering the tomb.

"This is my final warning, Ben—" Dr Fielding said. "For the sake of everyone here . . ." He motioned with one hand to the four workers.

"Superstition," Uncle Ben replied. "I cannot be stopped by superstition. I am a scientist." He raised the chisel and hammer. "The seal will be broken."

Dr Fielding tossed up both hands in disgust. "I will not be a party to this," he declared. He spun round, nearly hitting his head on the tunnel ceiling. Then, muttering to himself, he hurried away, disappearing quickly into the darkness of the tunnel.

Uncle Ben took a couple of steps after him. "Omar—? Omar?"

But we could hear Dr Fielding's footsteps growing fainter as he made his way out of the pyramid.

Uncle Ben sighed and leaned close to me. "I don't trust that man," he muttered. "He doesn't really care about the old superstitions. He wants to steal this discovery for himself. That's why he tried to make me stop outside the door."

I didn't know how to reply. My uncle's words startled me. I thought scientists had rules about who took credit for what discoveries.

Uncle Ben whispered something to Nila. Then he made his way back to the four workers. "If any of you agree with Dr Fielding," he told them, "you are free to leave now."

The workers exchanged glances with one another.

"You have all heard the words of warning on

the tomb door. I do not want to force anyone to enter the tomb," Uncle Ben told them.

"But we have worked so hard," one of the men said. "We cannot stop here. We have no choice. We *have* to open that door."

A smile crossed my uncle's face. "I agree," he said, turning back to the lion seal.

I glanced at Sari and realized that she was already staring at me. "Gabe, if you're scared, Daddy will let you leave," she whispered. "You don't have to be embarrassed."

She never quits!

"I'm staying," I whispered back. "But if you want me to walk you back to the tent, I will."

A loud *clink* made us both turn back to the door. Uncle Ben was working to prise off the gold lion seal. Nila had her camera poised. The workers stood tensely, watching Uncle Ben's every move.

Uncle Ben worked slowly, carefully. He slid the chisel behind the ancient seal and gently prised and scraped.

A few minutes later, the seal fell into my uncle's hands. Nila busily snapped photograph after photograph. Uncle Ben carefully passed it to one of the workers. "That's not a Christmas gift," he joked. "I'm keeping that for my mantelpiece!"

Everyone laughed.

Uncle Ben gripped the edge of the door with both hands. "I'm going in first," he announced. "If I'm not back in twenty minutes, go and tell Dr Fielding he was right!"

More laughter.

Two of the workers moved to help Uncle Ben slide open the door. They pressed their shoulders against it, straining hard.

The door didn't budge.

"It might need a little oiling," Uncle Ben joked. "After all, it's been closed for four thousand years."

They worked for several minutes with picks and chisels, carefully freeing the door. Then they tried once again, pressing their shoulders against the heavy mahogany door.

"Yes!" Uncle Ben cried out as the door slid an inch.

Then another inch. Another inch.

Everyone pressed forward, eager to get a view of the ancient tomb.

Two of the workers moved the large spotlights, aiming them into the doorway.

As Uncle Ben and his two helpers pushed against the door, Sari and I stepped up beside Nila. "Isn't this amazing!" Nila cried excitedly. "I can't believe I'm the only reporter here! I'm so lucky!"

I'm lucky, too, I realized. How many kids would give anything to be standing right where

I am? How many kids would *love* to be one of the first people in the world to step into a four-thousand-year-old tomb in an Egyptian pyramid?

The faces of some of my friends back home suddenly popped into my mind. I realized I couldn't *wait* to tell them about my adventure here!

The door scraped noisily against the dirt floor. Another inch. Another inch.

The opening was almost big enough for a person to squeeze through.

"Move the light a little," Uncle Ben instructed. "Another few inches, and we can go in and shake hands with the prince."

The door scraped open another inch. With a great heave, Uncle Ben and his helpers forced it open another few inches.

"Yes!" he cried happily.

Nila snapped a photograph.

We all pressed forward eagerly.

Uncle Ben slid through the opening first.

Sari bumped me out of the way and cut in front of me.

My heart was pounding hard. My hands were suddenly ice cold.

I didn't care who went in first. I just wanted to go in!

One by one, we slipped into the ancient chamber.

Finally, my turn came. I took a deep breath, slipped through the opening, and saw—

—nothing.

Except for a lot of cobwebs, the chamber was bare.

Totally bare.

I let out a long sigh. Poor Uncle Ben. All that work for nothing. I felt so disappointed.

I glanced around the bare chamber. The spotlights made the thick cobwebs glow like silver. Our shadows stretched across the dirt floor like ghosts.

I turned to Uncle Ben, expecting him to be disappointed, too. But to my surprise, he had a smile on his face. "Move the lights," he told one of the workers. "And bring the tools. We have another seal to remove."

He pointed across the empty room to the back wall. In the grey light, I could make out the outline of the door. Another sculpted lion sealed it shut.

"I *knew* this wasn't the real burial chamber!" Sari cried, grinning at me.

"As I said, the Egyptians often did this," Uncle Ben explained. "They built several false chambers to hide the real chamber from grave robbers." He pulled off his hard hat and scratched his hair. "In fact," he continued, "we may find several empty chambers before we find Prince Khor-Ru's resting place."

Nila snapped a photo of Uncle Ben examining the newly discovered door. She smiled at me. "You should have seen the expression on your face, Gabe," she said. "You looked so disappointed."

"I thought—" I started. But the scrape of Uncle Ben's chisel against the seal made me stop.

We all turned to watch him work at the seal. Staring across the cobweb-filled chamber, I tried to imagine what waited for us on the other side of the door.

Another empty chamber? Or a four-thousand-year-old Egyptian prince, surrounded by all of his treasures and belongings?

Work on the door went slowly. We all broke for lunch and then returned. That afternoon Uncle Ben and his helpers worked for another couple of hours, carefully trying to remove the seal without damaging it.

As they worked, Sari and I sat on the floor and watched. The air was hot and a bit sour. I suppose it was ancient air. Sari and I talked about last summer and the adventures we'd had in the Great Pyramid. Nila snapped our picture.

"Almost got it," Uncle Ben announced.

We all started to get excited again. Sari and I climbed to our feet and crossed the room to get a better view.

The lion seal slid free from the door. Two of the workers placed it gently into a padded crate. Then Uncle Ben and the other two workers set to work pushing open the door.

This door proved even more difficult than the last. "It's . . . really . . . stuck," Uncle Ben groaned. He and the workers pulled out more tools and began prising and chipping away the hard crust that had formed on the doorway over the centuries.

An hour later, they got the door to slide an inch. Then another inch. Another.

When it had slid halfway open, Uncle Ben removed the light from his helmet and beamed it through the opening. He peered into the next chamber for the longest time without saying a word.

Sari and I moved closer. My heart began racing again.

What did he see? I wondered. What was he staring at so silently?

Finally, Uncle Ben lowered the light and turned back to us. "We've made a big mistake," he said quietly.

A shocked silence fell over the room. I swallowed hard, stunned by my uncle's words.

But then a broad smile crossed his face. "We made a mistake by underestimating our discovery!" he exclaimed. "This will be more important than the discovery of King Tut! This tomb is even grander!"

A gleeful cheer echoed against the stone walls. The workers rushed forward to shake Uncle Ben's hand and offer their congratulations.

"Congratulations to us all!" Uncle Ben declared happily.

We were all laughing and talking excitedly as we slipped through the narrow opening, into the next chamber.

As the lights beamed over the vast room, I knew I was seeing something I would never forget. Even the thick layer of dust and cobwebs could not cover the amazing treasures that filled the chamber.

My eyes darted quickly around. I struggled to focus on it all. But there was too much to see! I actually felt dizzy.

The walls were covered from floor to ceiling with hieroglyphics, etched into the stone. The floor was cluttered with furniture and other objects. It looked more like someone's attic or a storeroom than a tomb!

A tall, straight-backed throne caught my eye. It had a golden, radiating sun etched into the seatback. Behind it, I saw chairs and benches, and a long couch.

Against the wall were stacked dozens of stone and clay jars. Some were cracked and broken. But many were in perfect condition.

A gold monkey's head lay on its side in the middle of the floor. Behind it, I saw several large chests.

Uncle Ben and one of the workers carefully pulled back the lid of one of the chests. Their eyes grew wide as they gaped inside.

"Jewellery!" Uncle Ben declared. "It's filled with gold jewellery!"

Sari came up beside me, an excited grin on her face.

"This is *awesome*!" I whispered.

She nodded agreement. "Awesome!"

We whispered in the heavy silence. No one else talked. Everyone was too overwhelmed by the amazing sight. The loudest sound was the clicking of Nila's camera.

Uncle Ben stepped between Sari and me and placed a hand on our shoulders. "Isn't this unbelievable?" he cried. "It's all in perfect condition. Untouched for four thousand years."

When I glanced up at him, I saw that he had tears in his eyes. This is the greatest moment of Uncle Ben's life, I realized.

"We must be very careful—" Uncle Ben started. But he stopped in mid-sentence, and I saw his expression change.

As he guided Sari and me across the room, I saw what he was staring at. A large stone mummy case, hidden in shadow, stood against the far wall.

"Oh, wow!" I murmured as we stepped up to it.

Made of smooth, grey stone, the heavy lid had a long crack down the centre.

"Is the prince buried inside it?" Sari asked eagerly.

It took Uncle Ben a moment to reply. He stood between us, his eyes locked on the ancient mummy case. "We'll soon see," he finally replied.

As he and the four workers struggled to move the lid, Nila lowered her camera and stepped forward to watch. Her green eyes stared intensely as the lid slowly slid away.

Inside was a coffin in the shape of the mummy. It wasn't very long. And it was narrower than I thought it would be.

The workers slowly prised open the coffin's lid. I gasped and grabbed Uncle Ben's hand as the mummy was revealed.

It looked so tiny and frail!

"Prince Khor-Ru," Uncle Ben muttered, staring down into the stone case.

The prince lay on his back, his slender arms crossed over his chest. Black tar had seeped through the bandages. The gauze had worn away from the head, revealing the tar-covered skull.

As I leaned over the case, my heart in my throat, the tar-blackened eyes seemed to stare helplessly up at me.

There's a real person inside there, I thought, feeling a chill run down my spine. He's about my size. And he died. And they covered him with hot tar and cloth. And he's been lying in this case for four thousand years.

A real person. A royal prince.

I stared at the stained, cracked tar that covered his face. At the gauze-like cloth, all frayed and yellowed. At the stiff body, so frail and small.

He was alive once, I thought. Did he ever dream that four thousand years later, people would open his coffin and stare at him? Stare at his mummified body?

I took a step back to catch my breath. It was *too* exciting.

I saw that Nila also had tears in her eyes. She rested both hands on the edge of the case and leaned over the prince's body, her eyes locked on the blackened face.

"These may be the best-preserved remains ever found," Uncle Ben said quietly. "Of course we will have to do many tests to determine the young man's identity. But, judging from everything else in this chamber, I think it's safe to say . . ."

His voice trailed off as we all heard sounds from the outer chamber. Footsteps. Voices.

I spun around towards the doorway as four black-uniformed police officers burst into the room. "Okay. Everybody take one step back," one of them ordered, lowering his hand to the gun holster at his side.

Startled cries filled the room. Uncle Ben spun round, his eyes wide with surprise. "What is happening?" he cried.

The four Cairo police officers, their features set in hard frowns, moved quietly into the centre of the room.

"Be careful!" Uncle Ben warned, standing in front of the mummy case as if protecting it. "Do not move anything. It is all terribly fragile."

He pulled off the hard hat. His eyes went from officer to officer. "What are you doing here?"

"I asked them to come," a voice boomed from the doorway.

Dr Fielding entered, a pleased expression on his face. His tiny eyes danced excitedly.

"Omar—I don't understand," Uncle Ben said, taking a few steps towards the other scientist.

"I thought it best to protect the contents of the room," Dr Fielding replied. He gazed quickly around the room, taking in the treasures. "Wonderful! This is wonderful!" he cried. He stepped forward and shook my uncle's hand enthusiastically. "Congratulations, everyone!" he boomed. "This is almost too much to believe."

Uncle Ben's expression softened. "I still do not understand the need for them," he said, motioning to the grim-faced officers. "No one in this room is about to steal anything."

"Certainly not," Dr Fielding replied, still squeezing Uncle Ben's hand. "Certainly not. But word will soon get out, Ben. And I thought we should be prepared to guard what we have found."

Uncle Ben eyed the four officers suspiciously. But then he shrugged his broad shoulders. "Perhaps you are right," he told Dr Fielding. "Perhaps you are being sensible."

"Just ignore them," Dr Fielding replied. He slapped my uncle on the back. "I owe you an apology, Ben. I was wrong to try to stop you before. As a scientist, I should have known better. We owed it to the world to open this tomb. I hope you'll forgive me. We have much to celebrate—don't we!"

"I don't trust him," Uncle Ben confided that

74

evening as we walked from the tent to dinner. "I don't trust my partner at all."

It was a clear night, surprisingly cool. The purple sky was dotted with a million twinkling white stars. A steady breeze made the palm trees sway on the horizon. The big campfire up ahead dipped and shifted with the wind.

"Is Dr Fielding coming with us to dinner?" Sari asked. She wore a pale green sweater, pulled down over black leggings.

Uncle Ben shook his head. "No, he hurried to phone Cairo. I think he's eager to tell our backers the good news."

"He seemed really excited when he saw the mummy and everything," I said, glancing at the pyramid rising darkly to the evening sky.

"Yes, he did," my uncle admitted. "He certainly changed his mind in a hurry! But I'm keeping my eye on him. Omar would like nothing better than to take over the project. I'm going to keep an eye on those police officers of his, too."

"Daddy, this should be a happy night," Sari scolded. "Let's not talk about Dr Fielding. Let's just talk about Prince Khor-Ru and how you're going to be rich and famous!"

Uncle Ben laughed. "It's a deal," he told her.

Nila was waiting for us by the campfire. Uncle

Ben had invited her to join us for a barbecue. She was wearing a white sweatshirt over loose-fitting jeans. Her amber pendant caught the light from the half-moon, just rising over the tents.

She looked really pretty. She flashed Uncle Ben a warm smile as we came near. I could tell by his face that he liked her.

"Sari, you're taller than Gabe, aren't you!" Nila commented.

Sari grinned. She loved being taller than me, even though I'm a little older.

"Less than an inch," I said quickly.

"People are definitely getting taller," Nila said to my uncle. "Prince Khor-Ru was so short. He'd be a midget today!"

"It makes you wonder why such short people built such tall pyramids," Uncle Ben said, grinning.

Nila smiled and took his arm.

Sari and I exchanged glances. I could see what Sari was thinking. Her expression said: What's up with those two?

We had a great dinner. Uncle Ben burned the hamburger rolls a little. But no one really minded.

Sari downed two hamburgers. I could only eat one. That gave her something else to boast about.

I was really getting fed up with my bragging

cousin. I found myself trying to think of a way to get back at her.

Nila and Uncle Ben kidded around a lot.

"That burial chamber looked like a film set," Nila teased my uncle. "It was all too perfect. All that gold. And that perfect little mummy. It's all a fake. That's what I'm going to write in my article."

Uncle Ben laughed. He turned to me. "Did you check out the mummy, Gabe? Was this one wearing a wristwatch?"

I shook my head. "No wristwatch."

"See?" Uncle Ben told Nila. "No wristwatch. So it's *got* to be real!"

"I guess that proves it," Nila said, smiling warmly at my uncle.

"Daddy, do you know the words to bring the mummy to life?" Sari broke in. "You know. The words on the tomb that Dr Fielding was talking about?"

Uncle Ben swallowed the last bite of his hamburger. He wiped the grease off his chin with a napkin. "I can't believe that a serious scientist would believe such superstition," he murmured.

"But what *are* the six words to bring the mummy to life?" Nila demanded. "Come on, Ben. Tell us."

Uncle Ben's smile faded. He shook his finger at Nila. "Oh, no!" he declared. "I don't trust you.

If I tell you the words, you'll bring the mummy back to life just to get a good photograph for your newspaper!"

We all laughed.

We were sitting around the campfire, its orange light flickering over our faces. Uncle Ben set his plate down on the ground and spread his hands over the fire.

"*Teki Kahru Teki Kahra Teki Khari!*" he chanted in a deep voice, waving his hands over the flames.

The fire crackled. A twig made a loud popping sound that made my heart skip a beat.

"Are those the secret words?" Sari demanded.

Uncle Ben nodded solemnly. "Those are the words of the hieroglyphs over the entrance to the tomb."

"So maybe the mummy just sat up and stretched?" Sari asked.

"I'd be very surprised," Uncle Ben replied, climbing to his feet. "You're forgetting, Sari—you have to chant the words five times."

"Oh." Sari stared thoughtfully into the fire.

I repeated the words in my mind. "*Teki Kahru Teki Kahra Teki Khari!*" I needed to memorize the words. I had a plan to scare Sari.

"Where are you going?" Nila asked my uncle.

"To the communications tent," he replied. "I have to make a phone call." He turned and made his way quickly over the sand towards the row of canvas tents.

Nila let out a surprised laugh. "He didn't even say good night."

"Daddy's always like that," Sari explained, "when he has something on his mind."

"Guess I'd better go, too," Nila said, climbing to her feet and brushing sand off her jeans. "I'm going to start writing my story for the paper."

She said good night and walked quickly away, her sandals making a slapping sound against the sand.

Sari and I sat staring into the crackling fire. The half-moon had floated high in the sky. Its pale light reflected off the top of the pyramid in the distance.

"Nila is right," I told Sari. "It really did look like a film set in there."

Sari didn't reply. She stared into the fire without blinking, thinking hard. Something in the fire popped again. The sound seemed to snap her out of her thoughts.

"Do you think Nila likes Daddy?" she asked me, her dark eyes locking on mine.

"Yeah, I think so," I replied. "She's always giving him this smile." I imitated Nila's smile. "And she's always kind of teasing him."

Sari thought about my reply. "And do you think Daddy likes her?"

I grinned. "For sure." I stood up. I was eager to get back to the tent. I wanted to scare Sari.

We walked towards the tents in silence. I guessed that Sari was still thinking about her dad and Nila.

The night air was cool, but it was warm inside the tent. Moonlight filtered through the canvas. Sari pulled her trunk out from under her camp bed and got down on her knees to search through her clothes.

"Sari," I whispered. "Dare me to recite the ancient words five times?"

"Huh?" She gazed up from the trunk.

"I'm going to chant the words five times," I told her. "You know. See if anything happens."

I expected her to beg me not to. I expected her to get scared and plead: "Please, Gabe—don't do it! Don't! It's too dangerous!"

But, instead, Sari turned back to her clothes trunk. "Hey. Give it a try," she told me.

"You sure?" I asked her.

"Yeah. Why not?" she replied, pulling out a pair of denim cut-offs.

I stared across the tent at her. Was that fear I saw in her eyes? Was she just pretending to be so casual about it?

Yes. I think Sari was a little scared. And trying hard not to show it.

I took a few steps closer and chanted the ancient words, in the same low voice Uncle Ben had used: "*Teki Kahru Teki Kahra Teki Khari!*"

Sari dropped the jeans and turned to watch me.

I repeated the chant a second time. "*Teki Kahru Teki Kahra Teki Khari!*"

A third time.

A fourth time.

I hesitated. I felt a cold breeze tingle the back of my neck.

Should I chant the words again? Should I go for number five?

16

I stared down at Sari.

She had closed the trunk lid and was leaning on it tensely, staring back at me. I could see that she was frightened. She chewed her bottom lip.

Should I chant the words for a fifth time?

I felt another chill at the back of my neck.

It's just superstition, I told myself. Four-thousand-year-old superstition.

There's no way that mouldy old mummified prince is going to come back to life just because I recite six words I don't even know the meaning of!

No way.

I suddenly thought of all the old films I had watched about mummies in ancient Egypt. In the films, the scientists always ignored ancient curses warning them not to disturb the mummies' tombs. Then the mummies always came to life to get their revenge. They staggered around, grabbed the scientists by the throat, and strangled them.

Stupid films. But I loved them.

Now, staring down at Sari, I saw that she was really scared.

I took a deep breath. I suddenly realized that I felt scared, too.

But it was too late. I had gone too far. I couldn't chicken out now.

"*Teki Kahru Teki Kahra Teki Khari!*" I shouted. The fifth time.

I froze—and waited. I don't know what I expected. A flash of lightning, maybe.

Sari climbed to her feet. She tugged at a strand of dark hair.

"Admit it. You're totally freaked," I said, unable to keep a grin from spreading across my face.

"No way!" she insisted. "Go ahead, Gabe. Chant the words again. Chant them a hundred times! You're not going to scare me! No way!"

But we both gasped when we suddenly saw a dark shadow roll over the tent wall.

And my heart completely stopped when a hoarse voice whispered into the tent: "*Are you in there?*"

My legs trembled as I stumbled back, closer to Sari.

I could see her eyes go wide with surprise—and fear.

The shadow moved quickly towards the tent opening.

We had no time to scream. No time to call for help.

Gaping into the darkness, I saw the flap pull open—and a smooth head poked into the tent.

"Ohhh." I let out a terrified moan as the dark figure slumped towards us.

The mummy is alive! The horrifying thought swept through my mind as I backed away. *The mummy is alive!*

"Dr Fielding!" Sari cried.

"Huh?" I squinted to see better.

Yes. It was Dr Fielding.

I struggled to say hello. But my heart was

pounding so hard, I couldn't speak. I took a long, deep breath and held it.

"I'm looking for your father," Dr Fielding told Sari. "I must see him at once. It's extremely urgent."

"He—he's making a phone call," Sari replied in a shaky voice.

Dr Fielding spun round and ducked out of the tent. The flap snapped shut behind him.

I turned to Sari, my heart still pounding. "He scared me to death!" I confessed. "I thought he was in Cairo. When he poked that skinny, bald head into the tent . . ."

Sari laughed. "He really looks like a mummy—doesn't he?" Her smile faded. "I wonder why he's in such a hurry to see Daddy."

"Let's follow him!" I urged. The idea just popped into my head.

"Yes! Let's go!" I hadn't expected Sari to agree so quickly. But she was already pushing open the tent flap.

I followed her out of the tent. The night had grown cooler. A steady wind made all of the tents appear to shiver.

"Which way did he go?" I whispered.

Sari pointed. "I think that's the communications tent at the end." She started jogging across the sand.

As we ran, the wind blew sand against our legs. I heard music and voices from one of the

85

tents. The workers were celebrating the day's discovery.

The moon cast a strip of light like a carpet along our path. Up ahead, I could see Dr Fielding's lanky body, leaning forward, lurching awkwardly towards the last tent.

He disappeared round the side of it. Sari and I stopped a few tents away. We ducked out of the moonlight, into deep shadows where we wouldn't be seen.

I could hear Dr Fielding's booming voice coming from the communications tent. He was talking rapidly, excitedly.

"What is he saying?" Sari whispered.

I couldn't make out the words.

A few seconds later, two figures emerged from the tent. Carrying bright torches, they crossed the strip of yellow moonlight, then moved quickly into shadow.

Dr Fielding appeared to be pulling Uncle Ben, pulling him towards the pyramid.

"What's going on?" Sari whispered, grabbing my sleeve. "Is he *forcing* Daddy to go with him?"

The wind swirled the sand around us. I shivered.

The two men were talking at the same time, shouting and gesturing with their torches. They're arguing about something, I realized.

Dr Fielding had a hand on Uncle Ben's

shoulder. Was he shoving Uncle Ben towards the pyramid? Or was Uncle Ben actually leading the way?

It was impossible to tell.

"Let's go," I whispered to Sari.

We stepped away from the tent and started to follow them. We walked slowly, keeping them in view, but being careful not to get too close.

"If they turn back, they'll see us," Sari whispered, huddling close to me as we crept over the sand.

She was right. There were no trees or bushes to hide behind here on the open desert.

"Maybe they won't turn back," I replied hopefully.

We crept closer. The pyramid rose up darkly in front of us.

We saw Dr Fielding and Uncle Ben stop at the opening in the side. I could hear their excited voices, but the wind carried away their words. They still seemed to be arguing.

Uncle Ben disappeared into the pyramid first. Dr Fielding went in right behind him.

"Did he shove Daddy in?" Sari demanded in a shrill, frightened voice. "It looked like he pushed him inside!"

"I—I don't know," I stammered.

We made our way closer to the entrance. Then we both stopped and stared into the darkness.

I knew we were both thinking the same thing. I knew we both had the same questions on our lips.

Should we follow them in?

Sari and I exchanged glances.

The pyramid seemed so much bigger at night, so much darker. The gusting wind howled around its walls, as if warning us to stay back.

We crept behind a pile of stones left by the workers. "Let's wait here for Daddy to come out," Sari suggested.

I didn't argue with her. We had no torches, no light of any kind. I didn't think we'd get very far wandering the dark tunnels by ourselves.

I pressed up against the smooth stones and stared at the pyramid opening. Sari gazed up at the half-moon. Thin wisps of cloud floated over it. The ground darkened in front of us.

"You don't think Daddy is in any kind of trouble, do you?" Sari asked. "I mean, he told us he didn't trust Dr Fielding. And then—"

"I'm sure Uncle Ben is okay," I told her. "I mean, Dr Fielding is a scientist. He's not a *criminal* or anything."

"But why did he force Daddy into the pyramid in the middle of the night?" Sari asked shrilly. "And what were they arguing about?"

I shrugged in reply. I didn't remember ever seeing Sari so frightened. Normally, I would have enjoyed it. She always bragged about how brave and fearless she was—especially compared to me.

But there was no way I could enjoy this. Mainly because I was just as scared as she was!

It *did* look as if the two scientists were fighting. And it *did* look as if Dr Fielding pushed Uncle Ben down into the pyramid.

Sari crossed her arms over her sweater again and narrowed her eyes at the opening. The wind fluttered her hair, blowing strands across her forehead. But she made no attempt to brush them away.

"What could be so important?" she demanded. "Why did they have to go into the pyramid now? Do you think something was stolen? Aren't those police officers from Cairo down there guarding the place?"

"I saw the four policemen leave," I told her. "They piled into their little car and drove away, just before dinner. I don't know why. Maybe they were called back to the city."

"I—I'm just confused," Sari admitted. "And worried. I didn't like the look on Dr Fielding's face. I didn't like the way he was so rude, just bursting into the tent like that. Scaring us to death. Not even saying hi."

"Calm down, Sari," I said softly. "Let's just wait. Everything will be okay."

She let out a sigh, but didn't say anything in reply.

We waited in silence. I don't know how much time went by. It seemed like hours and hours.

The shivers of cloud drifted away from the moon. The wind continued to howl eerily around the side of the pyramid.

"Where *are* they? What are they *doing* in there?" Sari demanded.

I started to reply—but stopped when I saw a flicker of light at the pyramid opening.

I grabbed Sari's arm. "Look—!" I whispered.

The light grew brighter. A figure emerged, pulling himself out quickly.

Dr Fielding.

As he stepped into the moonlight, I caught the strange expression on his face. His tiny black eyes were wide and seemed to be rolling around crazily in his head. His eyebrows twitched. His mouth was twisted open. He seemed to be breathing hard.

Dr Fielding brushed himself off with his hands and began walking away from the pyramid. He was half-walking, half-staggering, taking long quick strides with his lanky legs.

"But—where's Daddy?" Sari whispered.

Leaning out from the rocks, I could see the pyramid opening clearly. No light flickered. No sign of Uncle Ben.

"He—he isn't coming out!" Sari stammered.

And before I could react, Sari leaped out from our hiding place behind the stones—and stepped into Dr Fielding's path.

"Dr Fielding," she cried loudly, "where is my dad?"

I pushed myself away from the stones and hurried after Sari. I could see Dr Fielding's eyes spinning wildly. He didn't answer her question.

"Where is my dad?" Sari repeated shrilly.

Dr Fielding acted as if he didn't see Sari. He stepped past her, walking stiffly, awkwardly, his arms straight down.

"Dr Fielding—?" Sari called after him.

He hurried through the darkness towards the row of tents.

Sari turned back to me, her features tight with fear. "He's done something to Daddy!" she cried. "I *know* he has!"

I turned back to the pyramid opening. Still dark and silent.

The only sound now was the howling of the wind around the stone pyramid wall.

"Dr Fielding totally ignored me!" Sari cried, her face revealing her anger. "He stormed past me as if I weren't here!"

"I—I know," I stammered weakly.

"And did you see the look on his face?" she demanded. "So evil. So totally evil!"

"Sari—" I started. "Maybe—"

"Gabe, we have to go and find Daddy!" Sari interrupted. She grabbed my arm and started pulling me to the pyramid opening. "Hurry!"

"No, Sari, wait!" I insisted, tugging out of her grasp. "We can't go stumbling around the pyramid in the dark. We'll just get lost. We'll never find Uncle Ben!"

"We'll go back to the tent and get lights,"

she replied. "Quick, Gabe—"

I raised a hand to stop her. "Wait here, Sari," I instructed. "Watch for your dad. Chances are, he'll be climbing out in a few moments. I'll run and get some torches."

Staring at the dark opening, she started to argue. But then she changed her mind and agreed to my plan.

My heart pounding, I ran all the way back to the tent. I stopped at the tent opening, and gazed down the row of tents, searching for Dr Fielding.

No sign of him.

In the tent, I grabbed up two torches. Then I went hurtling back to the pyramid. *Please*, I begged silently as I ran. *Please be out of the pyramid, Uncle Ben. Please be safe.*

But as I frantically made my way over the sand, I could see Sari standing by herself. Even from a distance, I could see her frightened expression as she paced tensely back and forth in front of the pyramid opening.

Uncle Ben, where are you? I wondered. Why haven't you come out of the pyramid? Are you okay?

Sari and I didn't say a word. There was no need.

We clicked on the torches, then made our way into the pyramid opening. It seemed much steeper than I remembered. I nearly lost my balance, lowering myself to the tunnel floor.

Our lights crisscrossed over the dirt floor. I raised mine to the low ceiling. Keeping the light high, I led the way through the curving tunnel.

Creeping along slowly, I trailed one hand against the wall to steady myself. The wall felt soft and crumbly. Sari kept on my heels, her bright beam of light playing over the floor in front of our feet.

She stopped suddenly as the tunnel curved into a small, empty chamber. "How do we know we're going in the right direction?" she asked, her voice a quivering whisper.

I shrugged, breathing hard. "I thought you knew your way," I murmured.

"I've only been down here with Daddy," she replied, her eyes over my shoulders, searching the empty chamber.

"We'll keep going until we find him," I told her, forcing myself to sound braver than I felt.

She stepped in front of me, shining the light over the chamber walls. "Daddy!" she shouted. "Daddy? Can you hear me?"

Her voice echoed down the tunnel. Even the echo sounded frightened.

We froze in place and listened for a reply.

Silence.

"Come on," I urged. I had to lower my head to step into the next narrow tunnel.

Where did it lead? Were we heading towards Prince Khor-Ru's tomb? Is that where we would find Uncle Ben?

Questions, questions. I tried to stop them from coming. But they filled my mind, pestering me, repeating, echoing in my head, as we followed the tunnel's curves.

"Daddy? Daddy—where *are* you?" Sari's cries became more frantic as we moved deeper and deeper into the pyramid.

The tunnel curved up steeply, then levelled off. Sari suddenly stopped. Startled, I bumped into her hard, nearly making her drop her torch. "Sorry," I whispered.

"Gabe, look—!" she cried, pointing her beam of light just ahead of her trainers. "Footprints!"

I lowered my eyes to the small circle of light. I could see a set of bootprints in the dirt. A heel and spiky bumps. "Work boots," I muttered.

She circled the floor with the light. There were several different prints in the dirt, heading in the same direction we were.

"Does this mean we're going the right way?" she asked.

"Maybe," I replied, studying the prints. "It's hard to tell whether these are new or old."

"Daddy?" Sari shouted eagerly. "Can you hear me?"

No reply.

She frowned and motioned for me to follow. Seeing the many sets of prints gave us new hope, and we moved faster, trailing our hands along the wall to steady ourselves as we made our way.

We both cried out happily when we realized we had reached the outer chamber to the tomb. Our lights played over the ancient hieroglyphs that covered the wall and the doorway.

"Daddy? Daddy?" Sari's voice cut through the heavy silence.

We darted through the empty chamber, then slipped through the opening that led to the tomb. The prince's burial chamber stretched out in front of us, dark and silent.

"Daddy? Daddy?" Sari tried again.

I shouted, too. "Uncle Ben? Are you here?"

Silence.

I swept my light over the room's clutter of treasures, over the heavy chests, the chairs, the clay jars piled in the corner.

"He isn't here," Sari choked out with a disappointed sob.

"Then where did Dr Fielding bring Uncle Ben?" I asked, thinking out loud. "There's nowhere else in the pyramid that they might come."

Sari's light came to rest on the large stone mummy case. Her eyes narrowed as she studied it.

"Uncle Ben!" I shouted frantically. "Are you in here somewhere?"

Sari grabbed my arm. "Gabe—look!" she cried. Her light remained on the mummy case.

I couldn't work out what she was trying to show me. "What about it?" I demanded.

"The lid," Sari murmured.

I gazed at the lid. The heavy stone slab covered the case tightly.

"The lid is closed," Sari continued, stepping away from me and towards the mummy case. Her light remained on the lid.

"Yeah. So?" I still didn't understand.

"When we all left this afternoon," Sari explained, "the lid was open. In fact, I remember Daddy telling the workers to leave the lid open for tonight."

"You're right!" I cried.

"Help me, Gabe," Sari pleaded, putting her torch down at her feet. "We have to open the mummy case."

I hesitated for a second, feeling a wave of cold fear run down my body. Then I took a deep breath and moved to help Sari.

She was already pushing the stone lid with both hands. I stepped up beside her and pushed, too. Pushed with all my might.

The stone slab slid more easily than I'd guessed.

Working together, Sari and I strained against the lid, pushing . . . pushing.

We moved it about a foot.

Then we both lowered our heads to peer into the mummy case—and gasped in horror.

"Daddy!" Sari shrieked.

Uncle Ben lay on his back, knees raised, hands at his sides, his eyes shut. Sari and I shoved the heavy stone lid open another foot.

"Is he—? Is he—?" Sari stammered.

I pressed my hand on his chest. His heart was thumping with a steady beat. "He's breathing," I told her.

I leaned into the mummy case. "Uncle Ben? Can you hear me? Uncle Ben?"

He didn't move.

I lifted his hand and squeezed it. It felt warm, but limp. "Uncle Ben? Wake up!" I shouted.

His eyes didn't open. I lowered the hand back to the bottom of the mummy case. "He's out cold," I murmured.

Sari stood behind me, both hands pressed against her cheeks. She stared down at Uncle Ben, her eyes wide with fear. "I—I don't believe this!" she cried in a tiny voice. "Dr Fielding left

Daddy here to suffocate! If we hadn't come along . . ." Her voice trailed off.

Uncle Ben let out a low groan.

Sari and I stared down at him hopefully. But he didn't open his eyes.

"We have to call the police," I told Sari. "We have to tell them about Dr Fielding."

"But we can't just leave Daddy here," Sari replied.

I started to reply—but a frightening thought burst into my mind. I felt a shudder of fear roll down my body. "Sari?" I started. "If Uncle Ben is lying in the mummy case . . . then where is the mummy?"

Her mouth dropped open. She stared back at me in stunned silence.

And then we both heard the footsteps.

Slow, scraping footsteps.

And saw the mummy stagger stiffly into the room.

I opened my mouth to scream—but no sound came out.

The mummy lurched stiffly through the chamber doorway. He stared straight ahead with his vacant, tarry eyes. Under the ancient layers of tar, the skull grinned at us.

Scrape. Scrape.

His feet dragged over the dirt floor, trailing shreds of decaying gauze. Slowly, he raised his arms, making a terrifying cracking sound.

Scrape. Scrape.

My throat tightened in terror. My entire body began to tremble.

I backed away from the mummy case. Sari stood frozen with her hands pressed against her cheeks. I grabbed her arm and pulled her back with me. "Sari—get back! Get back!" I whispered.

She stared in terror at the approaching mummy. I couldn't tell if she heard me or not.

I tugged her back further.

Our backs hit the chamber wall.

The mummy scraped closer. Closer. Staring at us through its vacant, blackened eye sockets, he reached for us with his yellowed, tar-encrusted hands.

Sari let out a shrill shriek.

"Run!" I screamed. "Sari—run!"

But our backs were pressed against the wall. The mummy blocked our path to the doorway.

Moving stiffly, awkwardly, the ancient corpse dragged itself closer.

"This is all my fault!" I declared in a trembling voice. "I said the words five times. I brought him back to life!"

"Wh-what can we do?" Sari cried in a hushed whisper.

I didn't have an answer. "Uncle Ben!" I shrieked desperately. "Uncle Ben—help us!"

But the mummy case remained silent. Even my frantic screams could not awaken my uncle.

Sari and I edged along the chamber wall, our eyes locked on the approaching mummy. Its bandaged feet scraped over the floor, sending up dark clouds of dust as it moved heavily towards us.

A sour smell rose over the room. The smell of a four-thousand-year-old corpse coming to life.

I pressed my back against the cold stone of the chamber wall, my mind racing. The mummy stopped at the mummy case, turned stiffly, and continued lurching towards us.

"Hey—!" I cried out as an idea burst into my mind.

My little mummy hand. The Summoner.

Why hadn't I thought of it before? It had saved us last summer by raising a group of ancient mummies from the dead.

Could it also summon them to stop? Could it make them die again?

If I raised the little mummy hand up to Prince Khor-Ru, would it stop him long enough for Sari and me to escape?

He was only seconds away from grabbing us.

It was worth a try.

I reached into my back jeans pocket for the mummy hand.

It was gone.

"No!" I uttered a surprised cry and frantically grabbed at my other pockets.

No mummy hand.

"Gabe—what's wrong?" Sari demanded.

"The mummy hand—it's gone!" I told her, my voice choked with panic.

Scrape. Scrape.

The foul odour grew stronger as the ancient mummy dragged nearer.

I was desperate to find my mummy hand. But I knew there was no time to think about it now.

"We've got to make a run for it," I told Sari. "The mummy is slow and stiff. If we can get past him . . ."

"But what about Daddy?" she cried. "We can't just leave him here."

"We have to," I told her. "We'll get help. We'll come back for him."

The mummy made a brittle crackling sound as

it stepped forward. The sound of an ancient bone breaking.

But it continued towards us, moving stiffly but steadily, its arms outstretched.

"Sari—run—*now*!" I screamed.

I gave her a hard shove to get her going.

The room blurred as I forced myself to move.

The mummy made another loud, cracking sound. It leaned its body forward, and reached out as we dodged around it.

I tried to duck under the mummy's outstretched hand. But I felt the scrape of its ancient fingers against the back of my neck—cold fingers, hard as a statue.

I knew it was a touch I would never forget.

My neck tingled. I lowered my head from his grasp—and plunged forward.

Sari let out low sobs as she ran. My heart raced as I hurried to catch up to her. I forced myself to run, but my legs felt so heavy, as if they were made of solid stone.

We were nearly to the doorway when we saw a flickering light.

Sari and I both cried out and skidded to a stop as a beam of light swept into the room. Behind the light, a figure stepped into the doorway.

Shielding my eyes from the sudden brightness, I squinted hard, eager to see who it was.

"Nila!" I cried as she raised the torch beam to the ceiling. "Nila—help us!" I choked out.

"He's come alive!" Sari shouted to her. "Nila— he's come alive!" She pointed back towards the mummy.

"Help us!" I screamed.

Nila's green eyes widened in surprise. "What can I do?" she asked. And then her expression changed quickly to anger. "What can I do about you two kids? You shouldn't be here. You're going to ruin everything!"

"Huh?" I cried out in surprise.

Nila stepped into the room. She raised her right hand.

In the dim light, I struggled to make out what she was holding up.

My little mummy hand!

She raised it towards the mummy. "Come to me, my brother!" Nila called.

"How did you get my mummy hand? What are you doing?" I demanded.

Nila ignored my questions. She held the torch in one hand. She gripped the little hand in the other, holding it up towards the approaching mummy.

"Come here, my brother!" she called, waving the hand, summoning the mummy. "It is I, Princess Nila!"

Its legs cracking, its brittle bones breaking inside the gauze wrappings, the mummy obediently dragged itself forward.

"Nila—stop it! What are you *doing*?" Sari shrieked.

But Nila continued to ignore us. "It is I, your sister!" she called to the mummy. A triumphant smile crossed her pretty face. Her green eyes sparkled like flashing emeralds in the darting light.

"I have waited so long for this day," Nila told

the mummy. "I have waited so many centuries, my brother, hoping that someday someone would uncover your tomb and we could be reunited."

Nila's face glowed with excitement. The little mummy hand trembled in her hand. "I have brought you back to life, my brother!" she called to the mummy. "I have waited for centuries. But it will be worth it. You and I will share all this treasure. And with our powers, we shall rule Egypt together—as we did four thousand years ago!"

She lowered her eyes to me. "Thank you, Gabe!" she cried. "Thank you for The Summoner! As soon as I saw it, I knew I had to have it. I knew it could bring my brother back to me! The ancient words weren't enough. I needed The Summoner, too!"

"Give it back!" I demanded, reaching out for it. "It's mine, Nila. Give it back."

A cruel laugh escaped her throat. "You won't be needing it, Gabe," she said softly.

She waved her hand at the mummy. "Destroy them, my brother!" she ordered. "Destroy them now! There can be no witnesses!"

"Nooo!" Sari shrieked. She and I both dived to the doorway. But Nila moved quickly to block our path.

I shoved my shoulder against her, trying to push her away like an American footballer. But

Nila held her ground with surprising strength.

"Nila—let us go!" Sari demanded, breathing hard.

Nila smiled and shook her head. "No witnesses," she murmured.

"Nila—we just want to get Daddy out of here. You can do what you want!" Sari insisted desperately.

Nila ignored her and raised her eyes to the mummy. "Destroy them both!" she called. "They cannot leave this tomb alive!"

Sari and I spun around to see the mummy lumbering towards us. Its blackened skull glowed in the dim light. It trailed long strips of yellowed gauze across the dirt floor as it dragged itself closer.

Closer.

I turned back to the door. Nila blocked the way. My eyes darted frantically around the chamber.

No way to escape.

No escape.

The mummy lurched towards Sari and me.

And reached out its cold, cold hands to obey Nila's cruel command.

Sari and I darted towards the door. But Nila blocked our escape.

Its vacant eyes gazing blindly at us, its jaw frozen in a hideous skeletal grin, the mummy hurtled towards us.

Raised its arms stiffly.

Stretched out its hand.

Dived at us with a final, desperate lurch.

And to my shock, reached past Sari and me—and wrapped its tarred hands around Nila's throat.

Her mouth opened in a choked cry of protest.

The mummy tilted back its head as it gripped her. Its tarred lips moved, and a dry cough cut through the air. And then the whispered words, dry as death, escaped the mummy's throat:

"*Let me . . . rest in peace!*"

Nila uttered a choked cry.

The mummy tightened its fierce grip on her throat.

I spun around and grabbed its arm. "Let her go!" I screamed.

A dry wheeze erupted from the blackened skull. Its hands tightened around Nila, bending her back, bending her towards the floor.

Nila's eyes shut in defeat. Her hands flew up helplessly. The torch and the mummy hand fell to the floor.

I grabbed my little mummy hand and shoved it into my jeans pocket. "Let go! Let go! Let go!" I shrieked. I leaped on to the mummy's back and tried to pull its hands from Nila's throat.

It let out a defiant roar, a harsh whisper of anger.

Then it heaved itself up straight and struggled to toss me off its shoulders.

I gasped, startled by the mummy's surprising strength.

As I started to slide off the mummy's bandaged back, I reached out my hand, grabbing desperately, grabbing air, trying not to fall.

My hand grabbed on to Nila's amber pendant.

"Hey—!" I cried out as the mummy gave a hard toss.

I tumbled off.

The pendant tore off its chain. It fell from my hand, crashed to the floor—and shattered.

"Noooooooooo!" Nila's horrified wail shook the walls.

The mummy froze.

Nila spun out of the mummy's grasp. Backed away. Her eyes wide with terror. "My life! My *life!*" she shrieked.

She bent and struggled to pick up shards of amber from the floor. But the pendant had shattered into a hundred tiny pieces.

"My life!" Nila wailed, staring at the smooth pieces in her palm. She raised her eyes to Sari and me. "I lived inside the pendant!" she cried. "At night, I crept inside. It kept me alive for over four thousand years! And now . . . now . . . ohhhhh . . ."

As her voice trailed off, Nila began to shrink. Her head, her arms, her entire body grew tinier . . . tinier . . . until she disappeared into her clothes.

And a few seconds later, as Sari and I gaped down in horror and shock, a black scarab crawled out from under the sweatshirt and jeans. The scarab moved unsteadily at first. Then it quickly scuttled away over the dirt floor, disappearing into the darkness.

"That—that beetle—" Sari stammered. "Is it Nila?"

I nodded. "I suppose so," I said, staring down at Nila's crumpled clothes.

"Do you think she was really an ancient Egyptian princess? Prince Khor-Ru's sister?" Sari murmured.

"It's all so weird," I replied. I was thinking

hard, trying to piece it all together, trying to make sense of what Nila had said.

"She must have returned to her scarab form every night," I told Sari, thinking out loud. "She crawled into the amber and slept inside it. It kept her alive—until . . ."

"Until you smashed the amber pendant," Sari whispered.

"Yes." I nodded. "It was an accident—" I started.

But I choked on my words as I felt a cold hand close on my shoulder.

And knew that the mummy had grabbed me from behind.

The hand rested on my shoulder. The cold seeped through my T-shirt. "Let go!" I screamed.

I spun around—and my heart skipped a beat. "Uncle Ben!" I cried.

"Daddy!" Sari leaped forward and threw her arms around him. "Daddy—you're okay!"

He pulled his hand off my shoulder and rubbed the back of his head. He blinked his eyes uncertainly and shook his head, still a little dazed.

Behind him, I saw the mummy standing hunched over, frozen. Lifeless once again.

"Whew. I'm still groggy," Uncle Ben said, sweeping a hand back through his thick, black hair. "What a close call."

"It's all my fault," I admitted. "I repeated the words five times, Uncle Ben. I didn't mean to bring the mummy back to life, but—"

A smile crossed my uncle's face. He lowered his arm around my shoulders. "You didn't do it,

Gabe," he said softly. "Nila got there first."

He sighed. "I didn't believe in the power of the chant," he said softly. "But I do now. Nila stole your mummy hand and chanted the ancient words. She used The Summoner to bring the mummy to life. Dr Fielding and I were both suspicious of her."

"You were?" I cried, surprised. "But I thought—"

"I became suspicious of Nila at dinner," Uncle Ben explained. "Remember? She asked me what were the *six* ancient words to bring the dead to life? Well, I had never revealed that there were six. So I wondered how Nila knew there were six words."

Uncle Ben put an arm around Sari's shoulders, too, and led us to the wall. Then he leaned his back against the wall, rubbing the back of his head.

"That's why I hurried to the communications tent straight after dinner," Uncle Ben continued. "I phoned the Cairo *Sun*. They had never heard of Nila at the newspaper. So I knew she was a fake."

"But we saw Dr Fielding pull you from the tent," Sari broke in. "We saw him force you into the pyramid, and—"

Uncle Ben chuckled. "You two aren't very good spies," he scolded. "Dr Fielding didn't force me to do anything. He had spotted Nila

116

sneaking into the pyramid. So he found me at the communications tent. And the two of us hurried to the pyramid to see what Nila was up to.

"We got there too late," Uncle Ben continued. "She had already brought the mummy to life. Dr Fielding and I tried to stop her. She hit me over the head with her torch. She dragged me to the mummy case. I guess she stuffed me inside."

He rubbed his head. "That's all I remember. Until now. Until I awoke and saw Nila turn into a scarab."

"We saw Dr Fielding hurry out of the pyramid," Sari reported. "He walked right past me. He had the weirdest look on his face, and—"

She stopped and her mouth dropped open. We all heard the sounds at the same time.

The scraping of feet on the floor outside the burial chamber.

My heart jumped to my throat. I grabbed Uncle Ben's arm.

The footsteps dragged closer.

More mummies.

More mummies brought to life, staggering towards the prince's tomb.

I reached into my jeans pocket for my little
mummy hand. Pressing my back against the
wall, I raised my eyes to the chamber doorway—
and waited.

Waited for the mummies to appear.

But to my surprise, Dr Fielding burst into the
room, followed by four dark-uniformed police
officers, hands at their gun holsters.

"Ben—are you okay?" Dr Fielding called to
my uncle. "Where is the young woman?"

"She . . . escaped," Uncle Ben told him.

How could he explain that she had turned into
a bug?

The police explored the chamber warily. Their
eyes came to rest on the mummy, frozen in place
near the doorway.

"I'm so glad you're okay, Ben," Dr Fielding
said, placing a hand warmly on Uncle Ben's
shoulder. Then he turned to Sari. "I'm afraid I
owe you an apology, Sari," he said, frowning.

"When I ran out of here, I must have been in shock. I remember seeing you outside the pyramid. But I don't remember saying anything to you."

"That's okay," Sari replied quietly.

"I'm really sorry if I frightened you," Dr Fielding told her. "Your dad had been knocked unconscious by that crazy young woman. And all I could think about was calling the police as fast as possible."

"Well, the excitement is over," Uncle Ben said, smiling. "Let's all get out of here."

We started towards the doorway, but a police officer interrupted. "Could I just ask one question?" he asked, staring at the upright mummy in the centre of the floor. "Did that mummy walk?"

"Of course not!" Uncle Ben replied quickly, a grin spreading over his face. "If it could walk, what would it be doing in *this* dump?"

Well, once again, I turned out to be the hero of the day. And, of course, later in the tent, I wasted no time in bragging about my courage to Sari.

Sari had no choice. She had to sit there and take it. After all, *I* was the one who had stopped the mummy and turned Nila back into a beetle by smashing her pendant.

"At least you're not too conceited!" Sari shot back, rolling her eyes.

119

Lame. Really lame.

"Well, that scarab crawled away and disappeared," she said. An evil smile crossed Sari's lips. "I bet that bug is waiting for you, Gabe. I bet it's waiting for you in your camp bed, waiting to bite you."

I laughed. "Sari, you'd say anything to try to scare me. You just can't stand the idea that *I'm* the hero!"

"You're right," she replied dryly. "I *can't* stand the idea. Good night, Gabe."

A few minutes later, I was in my pyjamas and ready for bed. What a night! What an amazing night!

As I slid into the bed and pulled up the covers, I knew it was a night I would never forget.

"Ouch!"

Phantom of the
Auditorium

A mysterious phantom haunted our school.

No one ever saw him. No one knew where he lived.

But he haunted our school for more than seventy years.

My best friend, Zeke, and I were the ones who found him. We found him while we were doing a school play about a phantom.

Our teacher told us that the play was cursed, but we didn't believe her. We thought it was all just a big joke.

But when I saw the Phantom for myself, I knew it was no joke. It was all true. Every bit of it.

The night we found the Phantom was the scariest night of our lives!

But I should start at the beginning.

My name is Brooke Rodgers, and I'm in the sixth grade at Woods Mill Middle School.

Zeke Matthews is my best friend. A lot of the

other girls think it's weird that my best friend is a boy, but I don't care. Zeke is cooler and funnier than any girls I know. He is also a big horror movie fan, like me.

Zeke and I have been best friends for nine years. We know just about everything about each other. For instance, I know that Zeke still wears Kermit the Frog pyjamas!

He hates it when I tell people that. His face always turns a bright shade of red. Then his freckles stand out even more.

Zeke hates his freckles almost as much as I hate my glasses. I don't know why he's so hung up over a couple of freckles. After a while, you hardly even notice them. And in the summer when he gets a tan, they practically disappear altogether.

I wish my glasses could disappear. They make me look so nerdy. But if I don't wear them, I walk into walls!

Some girls at school think Zeke is cute. I never think about him that way. I guess it's because I've known him for nearly my entire life. Ever since our mums met in their bowling league and discovered they lived on the same street.

The excitement about the Phantom started a couple of Fridays ago. School had ended for the day, and I was trying to get my locker open. I pushed my hair off my face and turned the

124

combination dial. The stupid lock always jams, and it drives me crazy.

After trying the combination four times, I finally got it open. I threw my books inside and slammed the door shut. No way was I dragging home any textbooks over the weekend. As of right this second, I was on holiday! Two whole days of no school.

Excellent.

Before I could turn around, a fist came whizzing by my ear and punched my locker with a loud bang!

"What's up, Brookie?" a voice called from behind me. "No homework this weekend?"

I didn't have to turn around to know who it was. Only one person in the whole world can ever get away with calling me Brookie.

I turned around to see Zeke's dopey grin. His blond hair, which was really long in the front and very short—almost shaved—at the back, fell over one eye.

I smiled, then stuck my tongue out at him.

"Real mature, Brookie," he muttered.

Then I flipped my eyelids up so they stayed that way. It's a really gross talent I have that usually makes people scream and gag.

Zeke didn't bat an eye. He has seen my eyelid trick at least a zillion times.

"Nope, no homework!" I replied. "No books. No nothing. I'm totally free this weekend."

Then I had a great idea. "Hey, Zeke," I said, "do you think Rich can take us to see the *Creature* festival tomorrow?"

I was dying to see the three *Creature* movies playing at the Cineplex. One was supposed to be in 3-D! Zeke and I go to scary movies all the time just to laugh at the scary parts. We have nerves of steel. We never get scared.

"Maybe," Zeke answered, brushing his hair away from his face. "But Rich is grounded. He can't use the car for a week."

Rich is Zeke's older brother. He spends most of his life being grounded.

Zeke shifted his backpack on to his other shoulder. "Forget about the *Creature* festival, Brooke. Aren't you forgetting something?" He narrowed his eyes at me. "Something big?"

I scrunched up my nose. Forgetting something? I couldn't think of a thing. "What?" I asked finally.

"Come on, Brookie! Think!"

I really had no idea what Zeke was talking about. I pulled my long hair into a ponytail and tied it together with the hair scrunchie that was on my wrist.

I always wear a hair scrunchie on each wrist. I like to be prepared. You never know when you're going to need a hair scrunchie.

"Really, Zeke, I don't know," I said, making a tight ponytail. "Why don't you just tell me?"

And that's when it hit me. "The cast list!" I yelled, slapping my forehead. How could I have forgotten? Zeke and I had been waiting two long weeks to find out if we had got parts in the school play.

"Come on! Let's check it out!" I grabbed hold of Zeke's flannel shirt-sleeve. And I pulled him all the way to the auditorium.

Zeke and I had both auditioned for the play. Last year, we had small parts in the musical *Guys and Dolls*. Ms Walker, our teacher, told us that the play this year was going to be scary.

That's all Zeke and I had to hear. We *had* to be in this play!

We found a big crowd of kids at the bulletin board. They were all trying to read the cast list at once.

I was so nervous! "I can't look, Zeke!" I cried. "You check, okay?"

"Yeah, no prob—"

"Wait! I'll do it!" I yelled, changing my mind. I do that a lot. Zeke says it drives him crazy.

I took a deep breath and pushed through the crowd of kids. Biting my left thumbnail, I crossed the fingers on my right hand and stared up at the list.

But when I saw what was posted up there, I nearly bit off my whole thumb!

127

Tacked on the board beside the cast list was a sign:

Attention Brooke Rodgers: Please report to Mr Levy's office. You have been suspended from school.

Suspended?

I gasped in shock.

Had Mr Levy found out that I was the one who let the gerbil loose in the teachers' lounge?

Suspended.

I felt sick to my stomach. My parents were going to be so horrified.

Then I heard giggling.

I spun around to find Zeke laughing his head off. Other kids were laughing, too.

I stared angrily at Zeke. "Did you put that sign up?"

"Of course!" he replied, laughing even harder.

He has a sick sense of humour.

"I didn't believe it for a second," I lied.

I turned back to the board to read the cast list. I had to read the list three times. I couldn't believe what I saw. "Zeke!" I shouted over the other kids' heads. "You and I—we're the stars!"

Zeke's mouth dropped open in surprise. Then

129

he grinned at me. "Yeah. For sure," he muttered, rolling his eyes.

"No. Really!" I cried. "We got the two biggest parts! Come check it out for yourself! You got the part of the Phantom!"

"No way!" Zeke still didn't believe me.

"She's telling the truth, Zeke," a girl behind me said. Tina Powell, a seventh-grader, pushed through the crowd.

I always get the feeling that Tina Powell doesn't like me very much. I have no idea why. I hardly even know her. But she always seems to be frowning at me. Like I have a piece of spinach caught on my tooth or something.

"Let me see that list!" Zeke demanded, pushing past everyone. "Wow! I *did* get the starring part!"

"I'm going to be Esmerelda," I read. "I wonder who Esmerelda is. Hey, maybe she's the Phantom's crazy old stepmother, or maybe she's the headless wife who comes back from the dead to—"

"Give it a rest, Brooke," Tina said, frowning at me. "Esmerelda is just the daughter of some guy who owns a theatre." She said it as if Esmerelda were a nothing part.

"Uh, what part did you get, Tina?" I asked.

Tina shifted uncomfortably. A few other kids turned to hear her reply.

"I'm *your* understudy!" she muttered, staring

down at the floor. "So if you get sick or something and you can't be in the show, I'll play the part of Esmerelda.

"I'm also in charge of all the scenery!" she boasted.

I wanted to say something mean and nasty, something to put Miss High-and-Mighty Tina Powell in her place in front of everybody. But I couldn't think of anything.

I'm not a mean, nasty person. And it's hard to think of mean, nasty things to say—even when I want to.

So I decided to ignore her. I was too excited about the play to let Tina Powell get to me.

I pulled on my denim jacket and swung my backpack over my shoulder. "Come on, Phantom," I said to Zeke. "Let's go haunt the neighbourhood!"

On Monday afternoon, we started rehearsing the play. Ms Walker, my teacher, was in charge.

She stood on the stage in the auditorium, staring down at us. She clutched a tall stack of scripts in her arms.

Ms Walker has curly red hair and pretty green eyes. She is very skinny, as skinny as a pencil. She is a very good teacher—a little too strict. But a good teacher.

Zeke and I chose two seats next to each other in the third row. I glanced around at the other

131

kids. Everyone was talking. Everyone seemed really excited.

"Do you know what this play is about?" Corey Sklar asked me. He was playing my father. I mean, Esmerelda's father. Corey has chestnut-brown hair like me. And he also wears glasses. Maybe that's why we were playing relatives.

"Beats me," I answered him with a shrug. "Nobody knows what the play is about. I just know it's supposed to be scary."

"I know what it's about!" Tina Powell announced loudly.

I turned around in my seat. "How do you know?" I demanded. "Ms Walker hasn't passed out the scripts yet."

"My great-grandfather went to Woods Mill Middle School a long, long time ago. He told me all about *The Phantom*," Tina bragged.

I started to tell Tina that nobody cared about her great-grandfather's dumb story. But then she added, "He also told me about the *curse* on the play!"

That shut everyone up. Even me.

Even Ms Walker was listening now.

Zeke nudged me, his eyes wide with excitement. "A curse?" he whispered happily. "Cool!"

I nodded. "Very cool," I muttered.

"My great-grandfather told me a really scary story about this play," Tina continued. "And he told me about a phantom in the school. A real phantom who—"

"Tina!" Ms Walker interrupted, stepping to the front of the stage. She peered down sharply at Tina. "I really don't think you should tell that story today."

"Huh? Why not?" I cried.

"Yeah. Why not?" Zeke joined in.

"I don't think this is a good time to listen to scary stories that may not be true," Ms Walker replied sternly. "Today I'm going to pass out the scripts, and—"

"Do you *know* the story?" Tina demanded.

"Yes, I've heard it," Ms Walker told her. "But I wish you would keep it to yourself, Tina. It's a very scary story. Very upsetting. And I really don't think—"

"Tell us! Tell us! Tell us!" Zeke started to chant.

And, instantly, we were all grinning up at our teacher and chanting loudly: "Tell us! Tell us! Tell us!"

Why didn't Ms Walker want us to hear the story? I wondered.

How scary could it be?

"Tell us! Tell us! Tell us!" we all continued to chant.

Ms Walker raised both hands for us to be silent.

But that only made us stamp our feet in time to our chanting.

"Tell us! Tell us! Tell us!"

"Okay!" she shouted finally. "Okay, I'll tell you the story. But, remember—it's just a story. I don't want you to get too scared."

"You can't scare *us*!" Zeke cried.

Everyone laughed. But I was staring hard at Ms Walker. I could see that she really didn't want us to know this story.

Ms Walker always said we could talk about anything we wanted to with her. I began to wonder why she didn't want to talk about the Phantom.

"The story starts seventy-two years ago," Ms Walker began, "the year Woods Mill Middle

134

School was first built. I guess Tina's great-grandfather was a student here that year."

"Yes, he was," Tina called out. "He was in the first class that went to this school. He told me there were only twenty-five kids in the whole school."

Ms Walker crossed her skinny arms over the front of her yellow sweater and continued her story. "The students wanted to put on a play. A boy was hunting around in the basement of the Old Woods Mill Library. He found a script down there. It was called *The Phantom.*

"It was a very scary play about a girl who is kidnapped by a mysterious phantom. The boy showed it to his teacher. The teacher decided it would be fun to perform the play. It would be a grand production with the best scary special effects they could create."

Zeke and I exchanged excited glances. The play had special effects! We loved special effects!

"Rehearsals for *The Phantom* began," Ms Walker continued. "The boy who had discovered the play at the library won the lead role of *The Phantom.*"

Everybody turned to look at Zeke. He smiled proudly, as if he had something to do with it.

"The practised the play after school every day," Ms Walker continued. "Everyone was having a really good time. Everyone was working

135.

really hard to make it a good play. It was all going smoothly, until—until—"

She hesitated.

"Tell us!" I called out loudly.

"Tell us! Tell us!" a few kids started chanting again.

"I want you all to remember this is just a story," Ms Walker said again. "There's no proof that it ever happened."

We all nodded.

Ms Walker cleared her throat, then continued. "On the night of the play, the kids were all in costume. Parents and friends filled the auditorium. *This* auditorium. The kids were really excited and nervous.

"Their teacher called them together to give them a pep talk. The play was about to start. But to everyone's surprise, the boy playing the Phantom was nowhere to be found."

Ms Walker began pacing back and forth on the stage as she continued the story. "They called to him. They looked for him backstage. But they couldn't find the Phantom, the star of the show.

"They spread out. They searched everywhere. But they couldn't find him. The boy had vanished.

"They searched for an hour," Ms Walker continued. "Everyone was so upset, so frightened. Especially the boy's parents.

"Finally, the teacher stepped out on-stage to

announce that the play could not go on. But before she could speak, a horrible scream rang out over the auditorium."

Ms Walker stopped pacing. "It was a frightening scream. People said it was like an animal howl.

"The teacher ran towards the sound. She called to the boy. But now there was only silence. A heavy silence. No more screams.

"Once again, the entire school was searched. But the boy was never found."

Ms Walker swallowed hard.

We were all silent. No one even breathed!

"He was never seen again," she repeated. "I guess you could say that the Phantom became a *real* phantom. He just disappeared. And the play was never performed."

She stopped pacing and stared out at us. Her eyes moved from seat to seat.

"Weird," someone behind me murmured.

"Do you think it's true?" I heard a boy whisper.

And then, beside me, Corey Sklar let out a gasp. "Oh, no!" he cried, pointing to the side door. "There he is! There's the Phantom!"

I turned—along with everyone else—and saw the hideous face of the Phantom, grinning at us from the doorway.

Corey Sklar screamed.

A lot of kids screamed. I think even Tina screamed.

The Phantom's face was twisted in an ugly grin. His bright red hair stood straight up on his head. One eyeball bulged out from its socket. Black stitches covered a deep scar that ran all the way down the side of his face.

"BOO!" the Phantom yelled, bursting into the aisle.

More screams.

I just laughed. I knew it was Zeke.

I had seen him wear that dumb mask before. He kept it in his locker in case he needed it.

"Zeke, give us a break!" I called.

He pulled the mask off by the hair. His face was red underneath it. Zeke grinned at everyone. He knew he had just pulled off a really good joke.

Kids were laughing now.

Someone threw an empty milk container at

Zeke. Another kid tried to trip Zeke as he headed back to his seat.

"Very funny, Zeke," Ms Walker said, rolling her eyes. "I hope we won't have any more visits from the Phantom!"

Zeke dropped back into the seat next to me.

"Why did you scare everyone like that?" I whispered.

"Felt like it." Zeke grinned back at me.

"So, will we be the first kids to perform this play?" Corey asked Ms Walker.

Our teacher nodded. "Yes, we will. After the boy disappeared seventy-two years ago, the school decided to destroy all the scripts and the scenery. But one copy of the script was kept, locked up in the school vault for all these years. And now *we're* going to perform *The Phantom* for the first time!"

Kids started talking excitedly. It took Ms Walker a while to quieten us down.

"Now listen," she said, putting her hands on her pencil-thin waist. "This was just a story. An old school legend. I'll bet even Tina's great-grandfather will tell you that it isn't true. I only told it to put you all in a horror mood."

"But what about the curse?" I shouted up to her. "Tina said there was a curse!"

"Yes," Tina called out. "My great-grandfather said the play is cursed. The Phantom won't let anyone perform it. Grandpa says the Phantom is still here in the school. The Phantom has been haunting the school for over seventy years! But no one has ever seen him."

"Excellent!" Zeke declared, his eyes lighting up.

Some kids laughed. Some kids looked kind of uncomfortable. Kind of scared.

"I told you, it's just a story," Ms Walker said. "Now, let's get down to business, okay? Who wants to help me pass the scripts out? I've made a copy for each of you. I want you to take them home and begin studying your parts."

Zeke and I practically fell over each other running up to the stage to help Ms Walker. She handed us each a stack of scripts. We climbed back down and started to hand them out. When I came to Corey, he pulled his hand back. "Wh-what if the curse is true?" he called up to Ms Walker.

"Corey, please," she insisted. "Enough talk about the Phantom and the curse, okay? We have a lot of work to do, and—"

She didn't finish.

Instead, she screamed.

I turned back to the stage, where Ms Walker had been standing a second before.

She was gone.

She had vanished into thin air.

The scripts fell from my hands.

I turned and made a dash for the stage. I heard kids shouting and crying out in surprise.

"She just disappeared!" I heard Corey utter.

"But that's *impossible*!" a girl shrieked.

Zeke and I scrambled on-stage together. "Ms Walker—where are you?" I called. "Ms Walker?"

Silence.

"Ms Walker? Can you hear me?" Zeke called.

Then I heard Ms Walker's faint cry for help. "I'm down here!" she called.

"Down where?" Zeke cried.

"Down here!"

Down below the stage? That's where her voice seemed to be coming from.

"Help me up!" Ms Walker called again.

What's going on here? I wondered. How come we can hear her, but we can't see her?

I was the first to spot the big, square hole in the stage. Zeke and the other kids gathered around it. I stepped to the edge of the opening and peered down.

Ms Walker stared up at me. She was standing on a small, square platform, five or six feet below the stage. "You'll have to raise the platform," she said.

"How do we bring it up?" Zeke asked.

"Press that peg. Over there on the stage," Ms Walker instructed. She pointed to a small wooden peg to the right of the trapdoor.

"Got it!" Zeke cried. He pushed down the peg. We heard a clanking sound. Then a grinding sound. Then a groaning sound.

Slowly, the platform came rising up. Ms Walker stepped off the platform. She grinned at us and brushed off the back of her blue sacks. "I forgot about the trapdoor," she said. "I could have broken a leg or something. But I think I'm okay."

We all gathered around. Zeke dropped down on his hands and knees, staring down at the trapdoor.

"I forgot to mention the best part about this play," Ms Walker told us. "This trapdoor was built for the first production of *The Phantom*. It was totally forgotten. It's never been used in a school play—until now!"

My mouth dropped open. A trapdoor! How awesome!

Ms Walker reached down and tugged Zeke

back from the opening. "Careful. You'll fall," she said. "I lowered the platform earlier. I forgot it was still down."

Zeke climbed to his feet. I could see he was really interested in the trapdoor.

"When *The Phantom* was first supposed to be performed," Ms Walker told us, "the school had this trapdoor built so that the Phantom could disappear or rise up from below. Back then, it was a very impressive special effect."

I turned my eyes to Zeke. He seemed about to explode with excitement. "Am I the only one who gets to use it in the play?" he asked eagerly. "Can I try it now? Please?"

"Not yet, Zeke," Ms Walker replied firmly. "I still need to have it checked out for safety reasons. Until it has been checked, I don't want anybody fooling with the trapdoor."

Zeke was already back on his hands and knees, inspecting the trapdoor.

Ms Walker cleared her throat loudly. "Is that clear? Zeke?" she asked.

Zeke glanced up. He sighed. "Yes, Ms Walker," he muttered.

"Good," Ms Walker said. "Now let's get back to our seats. I'd like to read through the play once before we leave today. Just to give you an idea of the story and the characters."

We returned to our seats. Zeke's expression caught my eye. I'd seen that look in his face before. His forehead was wrinkled, and his left eyebrow was up. I could tell he was deep in thought.

It took more than an hour to read through the play. *The Phantom* was a really scary play!

It was about a man named Carlo who owns a very old theatre where plays and concerts are performed. Carlo thinks his theatre is haunted.

It turns out that there really is a phantom living in the basement. His face is scarred. He looks like a monster. So he wears a mask. But Carlo's daughter, Esmerelda, falls in love with the Phantom. She plans to run away with him. But her handsome boyfriend, Eric, finds out.

Eric is in love with Esmerelda. He tracks down the Phantom in his secret home in a dark passage far beneath the theatre. They fight. And Eric kills the Phantom.

This breaks Esmerelda's heart. She runs away, never to be seen again. And the Phantom survives as a ghost. He will haunt the theatre for ever.

Pretty dramatic, huh?

I think we all enjoyed reading through the play. We could see that it was going to be a lot of fun to perform.

When I read my lines as Esmerelda, I tried to picture what it would be like to be in costume, saying the lines on-stage. Once, I glanced back and saw Tina mouthing my lines silently to herself.

She stopped when she caught me watching her. She frowned at me the way she always does.

Tina is totally jealous, I told myself. She really wants to be Esmerelda.

For a moment, I felt bad for Tina. I didn't like Tina very much. But I didn't want her to *hate* me because I had the part she wanted to play.

But I didn't have much time to think about Tina. I had a lot of lines to read. Esmerelda was on-stage a lot in this play. It was a really big part.

When we finally finished reading the play, we all clapped and cheered.

"Okay. Go home, everyone," Ms Walker instructed, waving us to the door. "Start learning your parts. We'll meet again tomorrow."

As I began to follow the other kids to the door, I felt a hand pull me back. I turned to find Zeke pulling me behind a wide concrete beam.

"Zeke—what are you doing?" I demanded.

He raised a finger to his lips. "Shhhh." His eyes were really excited. "Let them all go," he whispered.

I peeked out from behind the pillar. Ms Walker lowered the lights. Then she collected her papers and made her way out through the auditorium door.

"Why are we hiding here?" I whispered impatiently.

Zeke grinned at me. "Let's try out the trapdoor," he whispered back.

"Huh?"

"Let's try it out. Quick. While there's no one in here."

I glanced quickly around the auditorium. Dark. And empty.

"Come on. Don't be a wimp," Zeke urged, pulling me towards the stage. "Let's try it out, okay? What could happen?"

I turned uncertainly to the stage. "Okay," I said.

Zeke was right. What could happen?

Zeke and I climbed on to the stage. It was darker than before. And it felt colder.

Our trainers thudded over the floorboards. Every sound seemed to echo over the whole auditorium.

"This trapdoor is so cool!" Zeke exclaimed. "Too bad you don't get to use it in the play."

I gave him a playful shove and started to reply. But I suddenly felt one of my sneezing attacks coming on. The dusty auditorium curtain must have triggered my allergies.

I have the worst allergies in creation. I am allergic to absolutely everything. You name it. Dust, pollen, cats, dogs—even some sweaters.

When I have an allergy attack, sometimes I sneeze thirteen or fourteen times in a row. My all-time record is seventeen.

Zeke likes to count my sneezes. He thinks he's a riot. He slaps the floor and yells, "Seven! Eight! Nine!"

147

Ha-ha. After ten sneezes in a row, I'm in no mood for jokes. I'm usually a pitiful, dripping mess with foggy glasses.

We tiptoed over to the trapdoor. "Check the floor around there," Zeke said quietly. "Find that peg that makes it work."

Zeke stood on the trapdoor while I searched for the peg in the darkness. I desperately tried to hold in my sneezes, but it wasn't easy.

Then the small peg on the stage floor caught my eye. "Hey—I've found it!" I shouted happily.

Zeke glanced nervously around the auditorium. "Ssshhh! Someone will hear you!"

"Sorry," I whispered. Then I realized I couldn't hold out any longer. My eyes were watering like crazy, and I just had to sneeze.

I grabbed a handful of tissues from my pocket and put the whole wad up to my nose. Then I started sneezing. I tried to keep them as silent as possible.

"Four! Five!" Zeke counted.

Luckily, it wasn't a record-breaking attack. I only made it to seven. I wiped my nose and shoved the dirty tissues in my pocket. It was gross, but I had nowhere else to throw them.

"Okay, Zeke, here goes!" I cried.

I stepped on the peg and jumped beside Zeke on the trapdoor.

We heard a clanking sound. Then a rumbling. Then a grinding.

The square section of floor began to lower itself.

Zeke grabbed my arm. "Hey—this thing is kind of shaky!" he cried.

"You're not scared—are you?" I challenged him.

"No way!" he insisted.

The clanking grew louder. The square platform shook beneath us as we slid down. Down, down—until the stage disappeared, and we were surrounded by darkness.

I expected the platform to come to a stop just beneath the stage. That's where it stopped for Ms Walker.

But, to my surprise, the platform kept dropping.

And it picked up speed as it slid farther and farther down.

"Hey—what's happening?" Zeke cried, holding on to my arm.

"How far down does this thing go?" I wondered out loud.

"Ohh!" Zeke and I both cried out as the platform finally hit the bottom with a hard *thud*!

We were both thrown to the floor.

I scrambled to my feet quickly. "Are you okay?"

"Yeah. I guess." Zeke definitely sounded scared.

We seemed to be in a long, black tunnel.

Dark. And silent.

I don't like to admit it. But I was very close to being scared, too.

Suddenly the silence was broken by a soft, raspy noise.

I felt panic choke my throat. That sound. What was it?

The sound repeated softly, steadily.

Like breathing.

My heart pounded in my chest. Yes! Breathing. The raspy breathing of a strange creature. So close to me.

Right next to me.

Zeke!

"Zeke—why are you breathing like that?" I demanded, feeling my heartbeat slow to normal.

"Breathing like what?" he whispered.

"Oh. Never mind," I muttered. He was breathing that way because he was scared. We were both scared. But there was no way we would ever admit it to each other.

We both raised our eyes to the auditorium ceiling. It was a small, square glow in the far distance. It seemed to be miles and miles above us.

Zeke turned to me. "Where do you think we are?"

150

"We're about a mile beneath the stage," I replied, feeling a chill.

"No kidding, Sherlock," Zeke replied nastily.

"If you're so smart, you tell *me*!" I challenged him.

"I don't think it's the basement," he said thoughtfully. "I think we're way below the basement."

"It feels like it's a big tunnel or something," I said, trying to keep my voice from shaking. "Want to explore?"

He didn't answer for a long moment. "Too dark to explore," he replied finally.

I didn't really want to explore. I was just pretending to be brave. Usually, I liked having the creeps. But being way down here was *too* creepy, even for me.

"We'll come back with torches," Zeke said softly.

"Yeah. Torches," I repeated. I didn't plan to *ever* come back!

I played nervously with the denim hair scrunchie on my wrist and stared out into the darkness. Something bothered me. Something didn't make sense.

"Zeke," I said thoughtfully, "why would the stage trapdoor come all the way down here?"

"I don't know. Maybe so the Phantom can get

home quicker after he haunts the auditorium!"
Zeke joked.

I punched him in the arm. "No jokes about the
Phantom—okay?"

If there really is a phantom, I told myself, *this
is where he would live.*

"Let's get out of here!" Zeke said, staring up at
the square of light so far above our heads. "I'm
going to be late for dinner."

"Yeah, sure," I replied, folding my arms
across my chest. "Just one question, Mr
Know-It-All."

"What question?" Zeke asked uncertainly.

"How do we get back up?"

We both thought about that one for a while.

After a minute or so, I saw Zeke drop to his
knees and begin running his hand along the
platform floor. "There's got to be a peg to push
down here," he said.

"No. The peg is up there," I replied, pointing
way up to the stage floor.

"Then there's got to be a switch or a lever or a
button to push!" Zeke cried. His voice grew high
and shrill.

"Where? Where could it be?" My voice sounded
just as shrill, just as frightened.

We both started feeling around in the darkness, feeling for something we could push, or
pull, or turn. Something to make the little square

platform rise up again and carry us back up to the auditorium.

But after a few minutes of desperate searching, I gave up.

"We're trapped down here, Zeke," I murmured. "We're trapped."

"This is all your fault," I muttered.

I don't know why I said that. I guess I was so frightened, I didn't know *what* I was saying.

Zeke forced a laugh. "Hey, I *like* it down here!" he boasted. "I may just stay down here for a while. You know. Do some exploring." He was trying to sound brave. But his voice came out tiny and trembling.

He wasn't fooling me. No way.

"How could you bring us down here?" I cried.

"You wanted to come, too!" he shot back.

"I did not!" I screamed. "Ms Walker *told* us this thing isn't safe! And now we'll be down here all night! Maybe for ever!"

"Unless we're eaten by rats!" Zeke joked.

"I'm *sick* of your stupid jokes!" I shouted. I totally lost it. I gave him a hard shove with both hands. He went sprawling off the platform.

It was so dark, I couldn't see him for a moment.

154

"Ow!" I cried out as he shoved me back.

Then I shoved him harder.

Then he shoved me harder than that.

I stumbled back—on to some kind of a switch. My back hit the switch.

A loud clanking sound made me nearly jump out of my skin.

"Brooke—jump back on! Quick!" Zeke screamed.

I leaped back on to the platform just as it started to move.

Up, up. Sliding slowly but steadily.

The square of light above our heads grew larger and brighter as we rose back up to the auditorium.

"Hey!" I cried out as the platform stopped with a jolt.

"Way to go, Brookie!" Zeke yelled happily. He slapped me on the back.

"Don't celebrate yet," I told him. We still weren't back on the stage. The platform had stopped about five feet down from the top. Just where it had been for Ms Walker.

I guessed that the only way to raise it all the way up was to step on the peg on stage.

"Give me a boost up," Zeke urged eagerly.

I cupped my hands together. He lowered his trainer into my hands.

"Wait!" he cried, stepping back down. "Whoa! What if the Phantom is up there waiting for

155

us? Maybe *you* should go first!"

"Ha-ha. Very funny," I said, rolling my eyes. "Remind me to laugh later."

"Okay, okay. I'll go first," he muttered.

He put his trainer into my cupped hands, reached up to the stage floor, and I gave him a boost.

I watched him scramble on to the stage. He disappeared from view.

I waited for him to reach down for me.

A whole minute went by.

"Zeke?" The word came out tiny and weak.

I waited some more. Listening hard.

I couldn't hear him up there. Where was he?

"Zeke? Where are you?" I called up. "Come on. Raise the platform. Or give me a hand," I called up. "I can't make it by myself."

Another minute passed. It seemed like an hour.

I suddenly realized what Zeke was trying to do.

That big jerk! He was trying to scare me!

"Hey! Enough!" I shouted.

I had had more than enough of Zeke Matthews for one day.

"Zeke!" I yelled. "Give me a break! Get me up!"

Finally, his hands lowered down over the side.

"It's about time!" I shouted angrily.

I grabbed both hands and let him pull me up to the stage.

I shook my hair back. My eyes were slowly adjusting to the brighter light. "You know, you're not funny!" I snapped. "Keeping me waiting down there was really—"

I stopped and swallowed hard. It wasn't Zeke who had pulled me from the trapdoor.

A strange pair of dark, angry eyes stared into mine.

I swallowed hard. A strange little man stared back at me, an angry scowl on his face. He wore baggy grey trousers and a loose-fitting grey sweatshirt, torn at the collar.

His thick white hair fell wild and unbrushed over his forehead like a floor mop. He had a deep purple scar down the side of his face, nearly as long as the scar on Zeke's creature mask.

I could see that he was old. But he was tiny, no bigger than a kid. He stood only three or four centimetres taller than Zeke.

As he squinted at me with his strange, grey eyes, his face twisted into an ugly frown.

He looks like a phantom! The frightening thought flashed through my mind.

"Wh-who are you?" I stammered.

"I'm Emile. The night janitor," the man rasped.

"Where's my friend Zeke?" I demanded in a shrill, frightened voice.

"Brooke, I'm over here," Zeke called out from behind me.

I whirled around. Zeke stood on the other side of the trapdoor. He had his hands shoved deep into his jeans pockets. He was biting his lower lip.

"Zeke!" I cried. "What's going on? Why—"

"The school is closed!" the janitor growled. He had a hoarse voice, like sandpaper. "What are you two doing in here?"

Zeke and I exchanged glances. Zeke took a step forward. "We . . . uh . . . stayed for play rehearsal," he told the man.

"That's right," I chimed in. "We had a late rehearsal."

The janitor continued to squint suspiciously at me. "Play rehearsal?" he repeated. "Then where is everybody else?"

I hesitated. This guy was scaring me so much, my legs wobbled. "We left," I blurted out. "But we had to come back to get my jacket."

Behind Emile, I saw Zeke nodding, approving my lie.

"How do you know about the trapdoor?" the janitor demanded in his sandpaper voice.

I hesitated. It's strange that I've never seen him in the school building before, I thought.

"Ms Walker, our teacher, showed it to us," Zeke said softly. I could see that he was as scared as I was.

The man leaned closer to me, squinting so that one side of his face was completely twisted up. "Don't you know how *dangerous* it is?" he whispered.

He leaned even closer, so close that I could feel his hot breath on my face. His pale grey eyes stared into mine. *"Don't you know how dangerous it is?"*

Zeke and I talked on the phone that night. "That man wasn't trying to *warn* us," I told Zeke. "He was trying to *scare* us."

"Well, he didn't scare *me* at all," Zeke boasted. "I'm sorry if he got *you* upset, Brookie."

Oh, wow, I thought. Sometimes Zeke is such a phoney.

"If you weren't scared, how come you were shaking all the way home?" I demanded.

"I wasn't shaking. I was just exercising," Zeke joked. "You know. Working out the calf muscles."

"Give me a break," I moaned. "How come we've never seen that janitor before?"

"Because he's *not* a janitor. He is . . . *the PHANTOM!*" Zeke cried in a deep, scary voice.

I didn't laugh. "Get serious," I told him. "It wasn't a joke. He was really trying to frighten us."

"Hope you don't have nightmares, Brookie," Zeke replied, laughing.

160

I hung up on him.

On Tuesday morning, I walked to school with my little brother, Jeremy. As we walked, I talked about the play.

I told Jeremy the whole story. But I left out the part about the trapdoor. Ms Walker said it would be better if we kept it a secret until the performance.

"Is it really scary?" Jeremy asked me. Jeremy is seven, and he gets scared if you say "boo" to him. Once, I made him watch the movie *Poltergeist* with me, and he woke up screaming every night for three weeks.

"Yeah, it's pretty scary," I told him. "But not scary like *Friday the 13th* scary."

Jeremy seemed relieved. He really hated scary things. On Hallowe'en, he hid in his room! I would never make him watch *Friday the 13th*. He would probably have nightmares till he was fifty!

"The play has a surprise," I added. "And it's a pretty awesome surprise."

"What is it?" Jeremy demanded.

I reached over and messed up his hair. It's chestnut-brown, like mine. "If I told you that," I said, making a funny voice, "it wouldn't be a surprise, would it?"

"You sound just like Mum!" Jeremy cried.

What an insult!

161

I dropped him off at his school and then crossed the street to my school. As I made my way down the hall, I thought about my part in the play. Esmerelda had so many lines. I wondered if I could memorize them all in time.

And I wondered if my old stage fright would come back. Last year, I had terrible stage fright in *Guys and Dolls*. And I didn't even have any lines to say!

I walked into the classroom, said good morning to some kids, made my way to my table—and stopped.

"Hey!" A boy I had never seen before was at my place.

He was kind of cute. He had dark brown hair and bright green eyes. He was wearing a big red-and-black flannel shirt over black jogging trousers.

He had made himself right at home. His books and notebooks were spread out. And he was tilting back in my chair with his black trainers resting on the table.

"You're in my place," I said, standing over him.

He gazed up at me with those green eyes. "No, I'm not," he replied casually. "This is *my* place."

"Excuse me?" I said, staring down at him.

He blushed. "I *think* this is where Ms Walker told me to sit." He glanced around nervously.

I saw an empty spot at the table behind mine. "She probably meant over there," I said, pointing. "I've been in this seat all year. Next to Zeke." I motioned to Zeke's chair. Zeke wasn't there. He was late, as usual.

The boy blushed even darker. "Sorry," he muttered shyly. "I hate being the new kid." He started to gather his books together.

"This is your first day?" I asked. I introduced myself.

"I'm Brian Colson," he replied, climbing to his feet. "My family just moved to Woods Mill. From Indiana."

I said I'd never been to Indiana. It was a boring thing to say, but it was true.

"You're Brooke Rodgers?" he asked, studying

163

me. "I heard you got the starring role. In the play."

"How did you hear that already?" I demanded.

"Some kids were talking about it on the bus. You must be a good actress, huh?" he added shyly.

"I guess. I don't know. Sometimes I get pretty bad stage fright," I told him.

I don't know why I told him all that. Sometimes I just rattle on. I guess that's why my parents call me Babbling Brooke.

Brian smiled shyly and sighed. "Back at my school in Indiana, I was in all the plays," he told me. "But I never had the lead role. I wish I had moved here sooner. Then I could have auditioned for *The Phantom*."

I tried to picture Brian on-stage in a play, but I couldn't. He didn't seem like the acting type to me. He seemed so shy. And he kept blushing all the time.

But I decided to give the poor guy a break. "Brian, why don't you come to rehearsal with me this afternoon?" I suggested. "Maybe you can get a small part or something."

Brian smiled as if I'd just offered him a million dollars. "You mean it?" he asked, wide-eyed.

"Sure," I replied. "No big deal."

Zeke came slinking into his seat, his eyes on Ms Walker's desk. "Am I late?" he whispered.

164

I shook my head. Then I started to introduce him to Brian. But Ms Walker stepped into the room and closed the door. Time for class to begin.

Brian hurried to his place at the other table. I started to sit down, but realized I'd left my science notebook in my locker.

"Be right back!" I called to Ms Walker. I hurried out of the door and jogged around the corner to my locker.

"Hey!" To my surprise, the locker door stood half open.

That's weird, I thought. I remembered locking it.

I pulled the door open the rest of the way. Started to reach inside for my notebook.

And let out a startled gasp.

Someone was in there—and he was staring right at me!

His ugly blue-and-green face grinned out at me.

I gasped again and clamped my hand over my mouth. Then I cracked up laughing.

Zeke and his dumb rubber creature mask.

"Well, you got me this time, Zeke!" I murmured out loud.

Then I saw the folded-up sheet of paper dangling beneath the mask. Some kind of note?

I pulled it out and unfolded it. Scribbled in red crayon was a message:

**STAY AWAY FROM MY
HOME SWEET HOME**

"Ha-ha," I murmured. "Very good, Zeke. Very amusing."

I pulled out my science notebook, slammed the locker shut, and locked it. Then I hurried back to the classroom.

Ms Walker stood behind her desk. She had just finished introducing Brian to everyone. Now she was reading the morning announcements. I slid into my seat beside Zeke. "You didn't scare me one bit," I lied.

He looked up from his maths notebook. Zeke always did his maths homework first thing in class. "Huh?" He flashed me his innocent look.

"Your mask," I whispered. "It didn't scare me."

"Mask? What mask?" he replied, tapping the pencil eraser against my arm.

I shoved him away. "Stop acting stupid," I said sharply. "Your note wasn't funny, either. You can do better than that."

"I didn't write you any note, Brooke," Zeke replied impatiently. "I don't know what you're talking about. Really."

"For sure," I said, rolling my eyes. "You don't know anything about the mask in my locker or the note, right?"

"Shut up and let me finish my maths," he said, staring down at his textbook. "You're not making any sense."

"Oh. Well. I guess the *real* Phantom did it, then," I said.

He ignored me. He was scribbling equations in his notebook.

What a phoney baloney! I thought. Zeke did it, and he knows it.

For sure.

After school, I led Brian to the auditorium. I practically had to drag him up on the stage. He was so shy!

"Ms Walker, are there any parts still available?" I asked. "Brian is really interested in being in the play."

Ms Walker glanced up from the script in her hands. I saw that she had scribbled notes all over the script. She studied Brian.

"I'm really sorry, Brian," she said, shaking her head. "You came to school a few days too late."

Brian blushed. I've never seen anyone blush so often.

"There aren't any speaking parts left," Ms Walker told him. "They've all been given out."

"Do you need a stand-in for anyone?" Brian asked. "I'm a very fast memorizer. I could memorize more than one part."

Wow, I thought. He really *is* eager to be in the play.

"Well, we really don't need any more stand-ins," Ms Walker told him. "But, I have an idea. You can join the scenery crew if you wish."

"Great!" Brian exclaimed with real enthusiasm.

"Go see Tina over there," Ms Walker told him, pointing to the group of kids meeting at the back wall of the stage. Tina was busily pointing out where she wanted the scenery to go, motioning dramatically with both hands, making everyone follow her all around the stage.

Brian seemed really happy. I watched him trot over to find Tina.

I took a seat in the auditorium and concentrated on my script. I was in practically every scene. How could I possibly memorize my whole part? I sighed and slouched back in the seat, slinging my feet over the seat in front of me.

I was memorizing my third line in the play, which went, "*What proof do you have that this man might be dangerous?*", when all the lights suddenly went out.

A total blackout! I couldn't see a thing.

Kids started to shout. "Hey! Who turned out the lights?"

"I can't see!"

"What's happening? Turn them back on!"

I sat straight up when I heard the shrill scream.

A terrifying scream—like an animal howl— that ripped through the darkness and exploded over the auditorium.

"No! Noooo!" I heard Corey Sklar moan.

And then I heard someone else cry out, "It's coming from up on the catwalk!"

Another shrill wail rose up over the frightened cries of my friends.

"Turn on the lights!" I heard Corey plead. "Please—turn on the lights!"

Other frightened voices called out, "Who is screaming?"

"Somebody—do something!"

"There's someone up on the catwalk!"

The auditorium lights flickered back on.

Another long howl from above the stage forced me to raise my eyes.

And I saw him. A green-and-blue masked creature wearing a shiny black cape.

Gripping a long, heavy rope, he came swinging down from high on the catwalk.

As he swung down to the stage, he threw his head back and laughed a horrifying evil laugh.

I jumped to my feet and stared in amazement.

The Phantom!

The Phantom landed hard on his feet. His shoes hit the stage floor with a *thud*.

He let go of the rope and it flew away from him.

The green-and-blue face glanced quickly around the stage. Tina and her scenery crew stood frozen against the wall, staring at him in horrified silence. Ms Walker appeared stunned. She had her arms tightly crossed over her chest.

The Phantom's cape swirled around him as he stomped one shoe on the stage.

He's short, I realized, standing and staring from down in the second row of seats. He's about Zeke's height. Maybe a few centimetres taller.

Or maybe he's *exactly* Zeke's height—because he *is* Zeke!

"Zeke! Hey—Zeke!" I called.

The ugly, masked face peered out to the auditorium. The Phantom started to sink. His feet disappeared. The legs of his dark trousers. Down. Down.

171

He had stepped on the peg and was riding the trapdoor down.

"Zeke!" I yelled. I ran up the aisle and pulled myself up on to the stage. "Zeke—you're not funny!" I shouted.

But the Phantom had vanished below the stage.

I ran up to the opening in the stage and stared down into the darkness. Ms Walker stepped up beside me, an angry scowl on her face. "Was that Zeke?" she asked me. "Was that really Zeke?"

"I—I'm not sure," I stammered. "I think so."

"Zeke!" Ms Walker called down into the opening. "Zeke—are you down there?"

No reply.

The platform had lowered all the way down. I couldn't see anything but a deep well of blackness.

Kids gathered around the opening, chattering excitedly, laughing and teasing each other. "Was that Zeke?" I heard Corey ask. "Was Zeke wearing that dumb mask again?"

"Is Zeke going to ruin our rehearsal today?" Ms Walker demanded angrily. "Does he think we *need* to be scared every afternoon?"

I shrugged. I couldn't answer.

"Maybe it wasn't Zeke," I heard Corey say. He sounded very frightened.

"It had to be Zeke. Zeke—are you here?" Ms Walker shouted, cupping her hands around her mouth. She turned slowly, her eyes darting over the stage and then all the seats of the auditorium. "Zeke Matthews? Can you hear me?"

No answer. No sign of Zeke.

"He's *your* friend, Brooke," Tina said nastily. "Don't you know where he is? Can't you tell him to stop ruining our play?"

I sputtered an answer. I was so angry, I didn't know what I was saying.

I mean, Zeke is my friend. But I'm not *responsible* for him!

Tina was just trying to make me look bad and score some points with Ms Walker.

"Okay, scenery people," Ms Walker instructed. "Back to work. I'll take care of this. The rest of you—"

She stopped. We all heard it. The loud clanking sound.

A loud hum rose up over the clanking.

"The trapdoor—it's coming back up!" I cried, pointing.

"Good," Ms Walker said, crossing her arms over her chest again. She narrowed her eyes at the opening in the stage floor. "Now I will let Zeke know how we feel about his little joke. His *last* little joke, if I have anything to say about it!"

Uh-oh, I thought. Poor Zeke.

Ms Walker was a really good teacher, and a really nice person, too—until you got on her bad side. But once you did that, once you made her angry, once you had her crossing her arms and squinting her eyes at you—the you were in major trouble.

Because she could be really mean.

I knew that Zeke was just having some fun. He loved being the centre of attention. And he loved to scare people. He especially loved to scare *me*.

This was a game for him, I knew. He was trying to show everyone that they were scaredy-cat wimps, and he wasn't.

Zeke played this game all the time.

But this time it had backfired. This time he had gone too far.

And Ms Walker was waiting for him, arms crossed, eyes squinting.

Will she throw him out of the play? I wondered. Or will she just yell at him until his ears curl?

The hum grew louder. The stage floor vibrated.

We all heard the platform stop—its usual five feet below the stage.

Poor Zeke, I thought. He's standing there innocently. He doesn't know what he's in for.

Poor Zeke.

I peered down into the opening—and gasped.

The platform was empty. No one there.

Zeke—or whoever it was—had sent it back up empty. And had disappeared into the dark tunnels far below the school.

Zeke wouldn't do that, I told myself. Even Zeke wouldn't be crazy enough to go down in that darkness by himself. Without a torch. Without a clue as to what was down there.

Would he?

Yes, he would. I answered my own question. If he thought he could *really* terrify us, Zeke would do anything!

Ms Walker cancelled the rehearsal. She told the scenery crew to stay and paint the backdrop. She told the rest of us to go home and study our parts.

"I'm going to have a long talk with Zeke when I find him," she muttered. Then she turned and made her way quickly out of the auditorium.

I took my time walking home. I thought about Zeke all the way. I was thinking so hard, I walked right past my house!

Down the block, I saw Zeke's mother's red Pontiac pull up their driveway. Shielding my eyes against the late afternoon sun, I saw Mrs Matthews climb out of the car. And then I saw Zeke on the other side.

"Hey! Zeke!" I shouted as I went running across the lawns towards him. "Zeke!"

His mother waved to me and disappeared into the house. Zeke looked surprised to see me. "Is play rehearsal over so early?" he asked.

"Yes. Thanks to you," I muttered.

"Huh?" He gave me his innocent look again. "What did *I* do?"

"You didn't scare me, Zeke," I told him. "No one thought it was funny. And now you're in a load of trouble with Ms Walker."

He narrowed his eyes and scrunched up his face, pretending not to understand. "What are you talking about, Brooke? How can I be in trouble? I wasn't even there!"

"You were there long enough," I told him.

He shook his head. His freckles seemed to grow darker. His blond hair fluttered in the wind. "No, I wasn't," he said quietly. "I *told* Ms Walker I wouldn't be there. I told her this morning that I had to miss rehearsal."

176

"So you could get into your mask and cape and come flying down from the catwalk?" I demanded suspiciously.

"No. I told her I had a dentist's appointment."

I gaped at him in shock. My mouth dropped open.

"What's your problem, Brooke?" he demanded. "It was only a check-up."

"You—you really weren't at school?" I stammered.

He shook his head. "No way."

"Then who was the Phantom?" I asked in a tiny voice.

A strange smile spread over Zeke's face.

"It *was* you!" I cried angrily. "You did your Phantom act, and *then* you went to your dentist's appointment! *Didn't* you, Zeke! *Didn't* you!"

He only laughed. He wouldn't answer.

After school the next afternoon, I walked with Brian to the auditorium. He looked cute in a black waistcoat over a plain white T-shirt and faded jeans. "How are you doing with Tina?" I asked.

"Okay, I guess," Brian replied. "She's a little bossy. But she's letting me design the backdrop pretty much on my own."

I waved to some kids who were heading out the door for home. We turned the corner. I saw Corey and Tina walking into the auditorium.

"Did Zeke work things out with Ms Walker?" Brian asked. "I saw him talking to her this morning."

"I guess," I replied. "She's letting Zeke stay in the play—for now."

"Do you think it was Zeke who pulled that stunt yesterday?" Brian asked.

I nodded. "Yes, I do. Zeke likes scaring people. He's been doing it since we were little. I think Zeke is trying to scare us. He's trying to make us think there's a real Phantom in the school." I smiled at Brian. "But I don't scare so easy!" I declared.

Soon after rehearsal started, Ms Walker called Zeke and me on-stage. She said she wanted to walk us through one of our scenes together. She wanted to show us where we should stand when we said our lines. She called it "blocking".

She also asked Tina Powell and Robert Hernandez, Zeke's understudy, to come up on-stage. Ms Walker said they should know all the blocking, too. Just in case.

Just in case? I thought. Then I remembered Tina's warning: *In case you get sick or something on the night of the play, I get to play your part.*

Well, Tina, I hate to disappoint you, I muttered

to myself, but I plan to be perfectly fine. So have fun painting your scenery. It's the only time you'll be on-stage.

I know, I know. That's kind of mean. But Tina deserved it.

Ms Walker showed Zeke where to stand. I stood off to the side of the stage with Tina, waiting for my cue to go on.

"I guess Ms Walker and Zeke worked things out," Tina said. "I heard him this morning telling her he was at the dentist's, and so he couldn't be the one to swing down from the ceiling."

I started to tell Tina to be quiet so I could hear my cue. But I was too late. I could already hear Ms Walker calling my name.

"Brooke Rodgers!" She sounded angry. "What's going on over there? You're supposed to be on-stage!"

"Thanks a bunch, Tina," I muttered under my breath. I ran out on to the stage. Glancing back, I could see Tina laughing to herself.

I couldn't believe it! Tina had made me miss my cue on purpose!

On-stage, I didn't know where I was supposed to stand. I didn't even know what page of the script we were on.

What was my next line?

I couldn't remember.

In a panic, I stared out at the kids in the

auditorium seats. They all stared back at me, waiting for me to speak.

I opened my mouth, but nothing came out.

"The line is, '*Is somebody down here?*'!" Tina yelled loudly from off-stage.

Oh, wow, I thought unhappily. Tina will do *anything* to show me up! She's just hoping Ms Walker will kick me out of the play.

I felt so angry, my head was spinning. I couldn't think straight. I repeated the line, then took a deep breath to calm down.

Zeke had the next line. He was supposed to appear on-stage and scare Esmerelda.

But Zeke wasn't on-stage. He wasn't anywhere in sight!

I peered out into the auditorium. Ms Walker stood at the front of the stage. She had her hands on her waist. She tapped one toe impatiently on the hard floor.

The auditorium grew silent, except for that tap. *Tap, tap, tap, tap, tap.* Ms Walker seemed to be *very* annoyed.

"Where is Zeke?" she asked wearily. "What is he doing now? Is he going to come flying down from the catwalk in full costume or something?"

I should have guessed what Zeke was up to. But it didn't dawn on me until I heard a familiar noise. The loud clanking. Followed by the hum.

The trapdoor platform! It was rising!

I sighed. "Here comes Zeke," I told Ms Walker.

And a second later, Zeke's blue-and-green masked head appeared.

I stepped back and watched him rise from down below. It looked awesome. Really dramatic.

Slowly, he appeared, rising up over the stage floor.

He reached the top and just stood there for a long moment, staring out at the auditorium, as if posing for a picture. He was in full costume: his mask, a black cape down to his ankles, black shirt and trousers.

What a ham! I thought. He really loves having everyone stare at him and think he's hot stuff!

And then he stepped towards me, taking quick strides. Through the mask, he raised his eyes to me.

I tried to remember what I was supposed to say next.

But before I could utter a sound, he grabbed both of my shoulders. He shook them really hard. Too hard.

Ease up, Zeke, I thought. It's only a rehearsal.

"*Go away!*" he cried in a furious whisper.

I remembered what I was supposed to say. I opened my mouth to speak . . .

But then I froze.

181

I saw someone waving to me from the edge of the stage.

Waving frantically.

It was Zeke!

I knew I was in major trouble.

If Zeke was standing way over there, who was shaking my shoulders, grinning at me through the ugly mask?

"*Help! Somebody-help me!*" I screamed, struggling to free myself.

"No, Brooke!" Ms Walker called out to me. "The line is, '*Help. Help me, Father.*'"

She didn't get it.

Couldn't she see that there was a *real* phantom up here trying to shake me to death?

Suddenly, the Phantom lowered his mask face and whispered harshly in my ear, "*Stay away. Stay away from my home sweet home!*"

I gazed into his eyes.

They looked familiar to me.

Who was he? I knew I'd seen him before.

But before I could remember, he spun away from me, took a diving leap off the stage, and ran up the long aisle, his cape flowing behind him.

I stood watching in horror as he disappeared out through the auditorium doors.

Some kids laughed. I heard Tina mutter to someone, "Was that in the script?"

Zeke came running over to me. "Brookie, are you all right?"

"I—I don't know," I replied. I felt really shaken up.

"That was *weird*!" Zeke exclaimed.

Ms Walker came striding across the stage, swinging her clipboard in one hand. She had a very confused expression on her face. "Can anyone explain what just happened here?" she asked.

"There's a real phantom in this school," Zeke said softly. He narrowed his eyes at me thoughtfully.

We were sitting in the front row of the auditorium. Brian scraped at a smudge of black paint on the back of his hand. I sat between the two boys, studying Zeke.

The lights had been dimmed. Rehearsal had ended a few minutes before. I could hear a few voices out in the hall. The door had just closed behind Ms Walker.

"Why are you staring at me like that?" Zeke demanded.

"I'm still wondering if you aren't responsible for *everything*," I told him bluntly.

He rolled his eyes. "Yeah. Sure," he muttered. "How could I be in two places at once today, Brooke? Answer me that. That's pretty tricky, even for someone as brilliant and clever as me!"

I laughed. "It's possible," I replied.

"I can't get this paint off," Brian moaned. "Look. I got it on my shirt, too."

"Is it washable paint?" Zeke asked.

"How should I know?" Brian replied unhappily. "I didn't read the label on the can. Do you read labels on cans?"

"Zeke only reads cereal boxes," I joked.

"Will you stop kidding around?" Zeke demanded impatiently. "We've got a real phantom in this school. And for some reason, he's trying to mess up our play."

I was still studying Zeke's face, trying to figure out if he was telling the truth. "I saw you talking to Andy Seltzer this morning before school," I told Zeke. "You could have planned this whole phantom thing with him. You gave Andy the costume, right? You told him what to do. You and Andy planned out the whole thing. Right?"

Zeke's mouth dropped open. "Huh? Why would I do that?"

"To scare me," I replied. "To scare everyone. To make us think there's a real phantom. And then when you get us really scared, you laugh and say '*gotcha!*' And we all feel like total jerks."

A smile crossed Zeke's face. "Wish I'd thought of that," he murmured. "But I'm serious, Brooke. I know you don't believe me, but I didn't plan anything with Andy. And I didn't—"

Tina hopped down from the stage. I guessed she'd been working on scenery behind the curtain. "Are you feeling better, Brooke?" she asked coldly.

I turned to her. "Feeling better? I'm okay. What do you mean?"

"You looked so stressed out on-stage, I thought maybe you were sick," Tina replied nastily. "Are you coming down with the flu? I hear there's a really bad one going around."

"I'm fine," I replied curtly.

"Is this paint washable?" Brian asked Tina.

Tina shrugged. "Beats me. Try turpentine." She smiled at Brian. "You're doing a good job on the backdrop." Then she turned back to me and her smile faded. "At least *someone* is doing a good job on this play."

Before I could reply, she turned and hurried across the aisle and out the auditorium door.

"She's *praying* I get the flu," I told Zeke. "Isn't that sick?"

He didn't reply. He was thinking so hard about the Phantom, I don't think he even heard me.

"Do you think Tina could be doing all these

terrible things?" I asked. "Just to frighten me away so she can be Esmerelda?"

"That's crazy," Zeke replied softly.

"Yeah. I guess," I agreed.

Brian just kept trying to peel the black paint off his hand.

"Let's go home," I suggested. "It's really late. Maybe we can talk about the Phantom later." I climbed to my feet.

Zeke glared up at me. "You still don't believe me—do you!" he accused. "You still think this is all some plot just to scare you."

"Maybe. Maybe not," I replied, climbing over him to get to the aisle. I really didn't know what to think.

Brian got up and followed me towards the door. I turned back to Zeke, who was still in his seat. "Are you coming? Are you going to walk with us?"

Zeke stood up without replying. "Yeah. I guess."

We were heading down the hall to our lockers when Zeke suddenly stopped. "Oh. I forgot," he uttered.

"Forgot what?" I asked. It was nearly dinner-time. I was eager to get home. My mum was probably wondering if I'd been run over by a bus or something. Mum always imagines me run over by a bus. I don't really know why. I never knew *anyone* who was ever run over by a bus!

187

"My maths book," Zeke said. "I have to go to the office. I left it in the auditorium the other night. I've got to see if anyone handed it in."

"I'll see you later," Brian said, backing down the hall.

"Where do you live?" I called to him.

He pointed in a direction. South, I think. "See you tomorrow!" He turned and jogged around the corner.

I followed Zeke to Mr Levy's office. All the lights were on, but the office was empty, except for Dot, the secretary. She was shutting down her computer, getting ready to go home.

"Did anyone hand in my maths book?" Zeke asked her, leaning on the counter.

"Maths book?" She squinted back at Zeke thoughtfully.

"I left it in the auditorium the other night," Zeke said. "I thought maybe that guy Emile turned it in."

Dot's expression turned to confusion. "Who? Who is Emile?"

"You know," Zeke replied. "The little old guy with the white hair. The night janitor."

Dot shook her head. "You're a little mixed up, Zeke," she said. "There's no one named Emile who works at the school. We don't *have* a night janitor."

Tina Powell called me at home that night. "Just wanted to see how you're feeling," she said. "You looked so pale, Brooke."

"I'm *not* getting the flu!" I shouted. I really lost my cool. But I couldn't help it.

"I heard you sneezing a lot yesterday," Tina said, pretending to be concerned.

"I always sneeze a lot," I replied. "'Bye, Tina."

"Who was that other phantom who jumped on-stage this afternoon?" Tina asked before I could hang up.

"I don't know," I said. "I really—"

"That was kind of scary," Tina interrupted. "I hope you weren't *too* scared or anything, Brooke."

"See you tomorrow, Tina," I said coldly.

I hung up the phone before she could say anything else. Tina was really becoming a pain, I decided.

How much does she want to play Esmerelda? I found myself wondering.

Just how much does she want the part? Enough to try to scare me away?

Zeke called later and convinced me that Emile *had* to be our phantom. "He lied to us, right?" Zeke asked excitedly. "He told us he worked for the school. And he tried to frighten us. It's *got* to be him," Zeke insisted.

"Yeah. Probably," I replied, twirling the hair scrunchie on my wrist.

"He's the right size," Zeke continued. "And he knew about the trapdoor." Zeke took a breath. "And why was he there, Brookie? Why was he there in the auditorium at night?"

"Because he's the Phantom?" I asked.

It made sense.

I agreed to get to school early so that Zeke and I could tell Ms Walker about Emile.

That night I dreamed about the play. I was on-stage in my costume. The spotlights were all on me. I stared out at the seats, filled with people.

The auditorium grew silent. Everyone was waiting for Esmerelda to speak.

I opened my mouth—and realized I didn't remember what I was supposed to say.

I stared out at the faces of the audience.

I had forgotten everything. Every word. Every line.

The words had all flown away, like birds leaving a nest.

My nest was empty. My mind was a total blank.

I stood there in panic. I couldn't move. I couldn't speak.

I woke up in a cold sweat. My entire body trembled. My muscles had all knotted up. I had kicked all the covers on to the floor.

What a horrible dream.

I couldn't wait to get dressed and get to school. I wanted to forget about that awful nightmare as quickly as I could.

I had to walk Jeremy to school. So I didn't get there as early as I wanted.

Jeremy kept asking me about the play. He wanted to hear more about the Phantom. But I really didn't feel like talking about it. I kept remembering my dream, remembering the panic of standing in front of three hundred people and looking like a total jerk.

I dropped Jeremy off, then hurried across the street. I found Zeke waiting for me by the front door. He was staring impatiently at his watch.

I don't know why. It doesn't have the correct time on it. It's one of those digital watches with seventeen different controls on it. Zeke can't figure out how to set it. He can play games on it—and play a dozen different songs. But he can't get it to tell the time.

191

"Sorry I'm late," I said.

He grabbed my arm and pulled me right into the classroom. He wouldn't even let me get my books from my locker or take off my coat.

We marched up to Ms Walker, who was sitting behind her desk, glancing over the morning announcements. She smiled at us, but her smile faded as she saw the solemn looks on our faces.

"Is something wrong?" Ms Walker asked.

"Could we speak to you?" Zeke whispered, glancing at the kids already in class. "In private?"

Ms Walker gazed up at the wall clock. "Can't it wait? The bell is going to ring in two minutes."

"It will only take a minute," Zeke promised.

She followed us out into the hall and leaned her back against the tile wall. "What's the problem?"

"There's a phantom in the school," Zeke told her breathlessly. "A real one. Brooke and I have seen him."

"Whoa!" Ms Walker murmured, raising both hands to say *stop*.

"No! Really!" I insisted. "We *did* see him, Ms Walker. In the auditorium. We sneaked in. To use the trapdoor, and—"

"You did *what*?" she cried, narrowing her eyes first at me, then at Zeke.

"I know, I know," Zeke said, blushing. "We weren't supposed to. But that's not the point."

"There's a phantom," I said. "And he's trying to stop the play."

"I know you think I've been doing all those things," Zeke added. "But I haven't. It's the Phantom. He—"

Ms Walker raised her hands again. She started to say something, but the bell rang—right over our heads.

We raised our hands to protect our ears.

When the bell finally stopped clanging, Ms Walker took a few steps towards the classroom door. It was really noisy inside. The kids were all taking advantage of her not being in there.

"I'm sorry I upset you with that story," she told us.

"Huh?" Zeke and I both cried out.

"I never should have told that old phantom story," Ms Walker said fretfully. "It got a lot of kids upset. I apologize for scaring you."

"But you didn't!" Zeke protested. "We saw a guy, and—"

"Have you been having nightmares about a phantom?" Ms Walker demanded.

She didn't believe us. She didn't believe a word we had said.

"Listen—" I started.

All three of us jumped when we heard a loud crash inside the room. A crash followed by wild laughter.

"Let's get inside," Ms Walker said. She

pointed at Zeke. "No more practical jokes—okay? No more jokes. We want the play to be good, don't we?"

Before we could answer, she turned and hurried into the room.

"What am I doing here?" Brian moaned. He shivered and stared up at the dark trees. "Why am I doing this?"

"You came with us because you're a nice guy," I told him, patting the shoulder of his sweater.

"No. Because I'm an *idiot*!" Brian corrected me.

This was all Zeke's idea. He came to my house after dinner. I told my parents we had our play rehearsal. A lie.

Then Zeke and I walked to school. We met Brian on the front walk, where he'd promised to wait for us.

"I can't believe Ms Walker didn't believe us," Zeke fretted.

"Would *you* believe such a nutty story?" I demanded.

"Well, we're going to find the Phantom and prove we're right," Zeke said firmly. "We have no choice now. I mean, if Ms Walker won't help us, we'll have to find him on our own."

"You just like a good adventure," I teased him.

He raised his eyes to mine. "Well, Brookie, if you're too scared. . ."

"But what am *I* doing here?" Brian repeated, staring at the dark school building.

"We need all the help we can get!" I told him. I gave Zeke a shove. "Let's go. I'll show you who's scared and who isn't."

"I think I'm a little scared," Brian admitted. "What if we get caught?"

"Who's going to catch us?" Zeke asked him. "You heard what Dot said in the office. There's no night janitor."

"But what if there's an alarm or something?" Brian demanded. "You know. A burglar alarm."

"For sure," I replied, rolling my eyes. "Our school can't even afford pencil sharpeners! No way they've got burglar alarms."

"Well, we're going to have to break in," Zeke said quietly, his eyes on the street. A car rolled by without slowing down. He tugged at the front doors again. "They're locked tight."

"Maybe a side door?" Brian suggested.

We crept around to the side of the building. The playground stretched out, silent and empty. The grass glowed all silvery under the bright half-moon.

The side doors were locked, too.

And the back door that led into the band room was also locked.

I raised my eyes to the roof. The building hovered over us like some kind of dark creature. The windows reflected the white moonlight. It was the only light I could see.

"Hey—that window is open!" Zeke whispered.

We ran full speed up to the half-open window in a ground-floor classroom. It was the home economics room, I saw. Mrs Lamston probably left the window open to let out the horrible smell of the muffins we baked that afternoon.

Zeke raised both hands to the window ledge and hoisted himself up. Sitting on the ledge, he pushed the window open wider.

A few seconds later, Brian and I followed him into the home economics room. The aroma of burned cranberry muffins lingered in the air. We tiptoed through the darkness to the door.

"Ouch!" I cried out as I banged my thigh into a low table.

"Be quiet!" Zeke scolded.

"Hey—I didn't do it on purpose!" I whispered back angrily.

He was already out the door. Brian and I followed, moving slowly, carefully.

The hall was even darker than the classroom. We kept pressed against the wall as we made our way towards the auditorium.

My heart was racing. I felt all tingly. My shoes scraped loudly over the hard floor.

Nothing to be afraid of, I told myself. It's just the school building, the building you've been in a million times. And there's no one else there.

Just you. Zeke. Brian. And a phantom.

196

A phantom who doesn't want to be found.

"I don't think I like this," Brian whispered as we edged our way around a corner. "I'm really pretty scared."

"Just pretend you're in a scary movie," I told him. "Pretend it's just a movie."

"But I don't *like* scary movies!" he protested.

"Ssshhh," Zeke warned. He stopped suddenly. I bumped right into him. "Try not to be a klutz, Brookie," he whispered.

"Try not to be a jerk, Zekey," I replied nastily.

I squinted into the darkness. We had reached the auditorium.

Zeke pulled open the nearest door. We peered inside. Total blackness. The air in the auditorium felt cooler.

Cool and damp.

That's because a *ghost* lives in here, I thought.

That made my heart pump even harder. I wished I could control my thoughts a little better.

Zeke fumbled with his hand against the wall and clicked on a row of lights over the section of seats to our left. The stage came into view. Empty and silent. Someone had left a ladder leaning against one wall. Several paint cans were lined up beside the ladder.

"How about turning on all the lights?" Brian suggested. He sounded really frightened.

"No way," Zeke replied, his eyes on the stage.

197

"We want to take the Phantom by surprise, don't we? We don't want to warn him that we're coming."

Huddled close together, we made our way slowly down the centre aisle towards the stage. In the dim light, long shadows fell over the seats.

Ghostly shadows, I thought.

Did a shadow move near the stage?

No.

Stop it, Brooke, I scolded myself. Don't let your imagination go wild. Not tonight.

I kept moving my eyes back and forth, checking out the stage and the rows of seats as we slowly made our way to the front.

Where is he? I wondered. Where is the Phantom?

Does he live in that dark chamber so far below the stage?

We were just a few feet from the stage when we heard the sound.

A footstep? A floorboard creaking?

All three of us stopped. All three of us heard it.

I grabbed Zeke's arm. I saw Brian's green eyes go wide with fright.

And then we heard another sound. A cough.

"We're . . . n-not alone!" I stammered.

"Wh-who's there?" I called. But my voice caught in my throat.

"Is anybody there?" Zeke called to the stage.

No reply.

Another footstep.

Brian took a step back. He grabbed the back of a seat and held on.

"He's back there," Zeke said, leaning close to me, his eyes excited. "I know he's back there."

"Where?" I demanded, choking out the word. It was hard to talk with my heart in my throat.

I stared up at the stage. I couldn't see anyone.

I jumped when I heard another cough.

And then a clanking sound rose up over the stage and echoed through the auditorium.

At first I thought the trapdoor was about to move.

Was someone riding up on it? Was the Phantom about to rise in front of our eyes?

No.

I cried out when I saw the backdrop begin to unfurl.

The clanking sound grew louder. The backdrop was slowly being lowered at the back of the stage.

"Who is doing it?" I whispered. "Who on earth is sending it down?"

Zeke and Brian stared straight ahead and didn't reply.

Zeke's mouth was wide open. His eyes didn't blink.

Brian gripped the back of the chair with both hands.

The painted backdrop clanked down, unrolling as it lowered.

All three of us gasped as we saw what had been done to it.

It had been a grey brick theatre wall. Brian and several other kids had worked for days on it, sketching it out, then painting it brick by brick.

"Who—who *did* that to my painting?" Brian cried out.

Zeke and I remained staring at it in silent horror.

The grey wall had been covered with red paint splotches and thick, red smears.

It looked as if someone had dipped a wide brush in red paint, then smeared and stabbed it all over the backdrop.

"It's ruined!" Brian declared shrilly.

Zeke was the first to move. He raised his hands to the stage floor and pulled himself up on to the stage. Brian and I followed after him.

"Who's here?" Zeke called out, cupping his hands around his mouth. "Who's in here?"

Silence.

Someone was here, I knew. *Someone* had to lower that backdrop so that we could see what had been done to it.

"Who's here? Where are you?" Zeke repeated.

Again, no reply.

We moved closer, making our way slowly, keeping close together.

And as we stepped up to it, words came into view. They were scrawled across the bottom, thick letters in heavy red paint.

I stopped and squinted to read the message in the dim light:

STAY AWAY FROM MY HOME SWEET HOME.

"Whoa," I murmured. I felt a chill roll down my back.

Then I heard a side door being pulled open.

All three of us turned away from the backdrop in time to see a figure step into the auditorium.

We cried out in surprise when we saw who it was.

201

She stood gaping up at us. She blinked her eyes
several times, as if she didn't believe what she
was seeing.

"I—I am really shocked," Ms Walker said
finally.

I swallowed hard. I struggled to say something, but no sound would come out.

Zeke and Brian stood frozen like me.

"I am so disappointed in all three of you," Ms
Walker said, stepping closer. "Breaking and
entering is a serious crime. And the three of you
have no business—"

She stopped short and let out a little gurgle as
her eyes fell on the backdrop. She had been so
surprised to find Zeke, Brian, and me on-stage,
she hadn't seen it—until now.

"Oh, no! Oh, good heavens!" she cried, raising
both hands to her face. She tilted. Sort of toppled
from side to side. I thought she was about to fall
over!

"How *could* you?" she gasped. She hurried across the stage, her eyes on the paint-splotched backdrop. "How could you ruin it? All the students worked for so many days to get it right. How could you ruin it for everyone?"

"We didn't," Zeke said quietly.

"We didn't do it," I repeated.

She shook her head hard, as if trying to shake us away. "I'm afraid I've caught you red-handed," she said quietly, almost sadly. I saw tears brim in her eyes.

"Ms Walker, really—" I started.

She raised a hand to stop me. "Was it so important to you three to have your little joke?" she asked, her voice trembling.

"Ms Walker—"

"Was it so important to make everyone believe there is a phantom? So important that you broke into the school—committed a serious crime—and then completely destroyed the scenery for our play? Was your joke so important?"

"We really didn't do it," I insisted, my voice trembling, too.

Ms Walker stepped forward and rubbed a finger over a red paint splotch on the backdrop. When she pulled the finger away, it was smeared with red paint.

"The paint is still wet," she said, her eyes burning accusingly into mine. "There's no one else here. Are you going to keep lying to me all night?"

"If you'd just give us a chance—" Zeke started.

"I'm especially disappointed in you, Brian," Ms Walker said, shaking her head, a frown tightening her features. "You just started at this school a week or so ago. You should be on your best behaviour."

Brian blushed redder than I've ever seen a human blush. He lowered his eyes, as if he were guilty.

I took a deep breath. "Ms Walker, you *have* to let us explain!" I cried shrilly. "We really didn't do this! We found it like this! Really!"

Ms Walker opened her mouth to speak, but changed her mind. "Okay." She crossed her arms over her skinny chest. "Go ahead. But I want the *truth*."

"The truth," I said. I raised my right hand, as if swearing an oath. "Brian, Zeke and I *did* sneak into the school. We didn't really break in. We climbed in through a window."

"Why?" Ms Walker demanded sternly. "What are you doing here? Why aren't you home where you should be?"

"We came to look for the Phantom," Zeke broke in. He swept his blond hair back with one hand. He always did that to his hair when he was really tense.

"We told you about the Phantom this

morning, but you didn't believe us."

"Of course I didn't believe you!" Ms Walker declared. "It's an old legend. Just a story." She frowned at Zeke.

Zeke let out a frustrated sigh. "We saw the Phantom, Ms Walker. Brooke and I. We saw him. He's the one who painted all over the backdrop. Not us. He's the one who swung down from the catwalk. And grabbed Brooke at rehearsal."

"Why should I believe that?" Ms Walker demanded, her arms still tightly crossed in front of her.

"Because it's true," I said. "Zeke, Brian and I—we came to the auditorium to look for the Phantom."

"Where were you going to look for him?" Ms Walker asked.

"Well," Zeke stammered. "Probably underneath the stage."

"You were going to take the trapdoor down?" Ms Walker asked.

I nodded. "Maybe. If we had to."

"But I clearly instructed everyone to stay away from the trapdoor," she said.

"I know," I told her. "And I'm sorry. We're all sorry. But we are really desperate to find the Phantom, to prove to you that he is real, that we're not making him up."

Her expression remained hard. She continued

to glare at us. "I haven't heard anything to convince me," she said.

"When we got here, we heard some noises," Zeke told her, shifting uncontrollably from foot to foot. "Footsteps. Floorboards creaking. So we knew someone else was here."

"And then the backdrop started to come down," Brian broke in, his voice shaky and small. "We just stood here and watched it, Ms Walker. That's the truth. And then when we saw how it was messed up, we ... we couldn't believe it!"

Ms Walker's expression softened a little. Brian sounded so upset, I think she was starting to believe him.

"I worked so hard on that backdrop," Brian continued. "It was the first thing I ever worked on at this school, and I wanted it to be good. I wouldn't wreck my own backdrop for a dumb joke. I really wouldn't."

Ms Walker uncrossed her arms. She glanced at each of us, then returned her eyes to the backdrop. Her lips silently formed the words of the scrawled message:

STAY AWAY FROM MY HOME SWEET HOME.

She shut her eyes and kept them shut for a long moment. Then she turned back to us. "I want to believe you," she confessed with a sigh. "But I just don't know."

She began to pace back and forth in front of us. "I drove back to school because I'd forgotten your maths test papers. I heard voices in the auditorium. I come in here, and I find you on the stage. The scenery totally smeared and destroyed. The paint still wet. And you ask me to believe that a mysterious phantom from over seventy years ago is responsible."

I didn't say a word. Neither did Zeke or Brian. I don't think we had anything more to say.

"The weird thing is, I'm starting to believe you," Ms Walker said, frowning.

The three of us let out relieved sighs.

"At least, I'm starting to believe that you didn't paint on the backdrop." She shook her hair hard. Her skinny body shuddered. "It's getting late," she said softly. "Let's all go home. I need to think about this. Maybe we need to ask Mr Levy for an investigation. Maybe he can help us find the culprit who is trying to ruin our play."

Oh, no, I thought. Not the principal. What if he decides to cancel our play? But I didn't say anything. None of us did. We didn't even look at one another. We followed Ms Walker out into the hall.

I was just so relieved that she had started to believe us. And that she was letting us go.

She clicked on a hall light so we could see our way.

We took a few steps, walking behind her.

Then we all stopped at once.

We all saw the red paint spots on the hall floor. A trail of red paint spots.

"Well, look at this!" Ms Walker declared. "Our painter was a little careless. He or she left a trail to follow."

She clicked on more lights.

We followed the red paint splotches down the long hall. We could clearly see a shoe print in one of the bigger paint puddles.

"I don't believe this!" Zeke whispered to me. "Someone left a trail."

"I'm glad," I whispered back. "Maybe the paint drips will lead us to the one who splotched up the backdrop."

"You mean the Phantom?" Zeke whispered.

We turned a corner. We passed a small paint smear.

"At least this will prove to Ms Walker that we're telling the truth," Brian said softly.

We turned another corner.

The paint trail stopped suddenly. One last tiny red puddle stood in front of a locker.

"Hmmmm," Ms Walker said thoughtfully, moving her eyes from the paint smear to the locker. "The trail seems to lead right to here."

"Hey!" Zeke cried out, startling all of us. I could see his eyes go wide with shock. "That's *my* locker!"

No one said anything for a moment.

I could hear Zeke's breaths, short and fast. I turned to him. He was staring at his locker, staring hard at the grey metal doors as if he could see inside.

"Open your locker, Zeke," Ms Walker instructed. She said it through gritted teeth.

"Huh?" Zeke gaped at her, as if he didn't understand what she meant. He lowered his eyes to the smear of red paint on the floor under his locker door.

"Go ahead. Open your locker," Ms Walker repeated patiently. She suddenly looked very tired.

Zeke hesitated. "But there's nothing in there," he protested. "Just books and notebooks and stuff."

"Please." Ms Walker motioned to the combination lock with one hand. "Please, Zeke. It's really late."

"But you don't think—?" Zeke started.

Ms Walker motioned to the lock again.

"Maybe somebody wanted to make it look like Zeke was the one with the paint," I suggested. "Maybe someone deliberately made that trail of paint lead to Zeke's locker."

"Maybe," Ms Walker replied calmly. "That's why I want him to open his locker."

"Okay, okay," Zeke muttered. His hand shook as he reached for the combination lock. He leaned his head forward and concentrated as he spun the dial, first one direction, then the other.

"Give me some light," he said edgily.

I backed up. "Sorry." I didn't realize I was standing in his light.

I glanced at Brian. He had his hands shoved in his pockets. He leaned against the wall and stared intently at Zeke's hands as Zeke twirled the lock.

Finally, Zeke pulled the lock open with a loud *click*.

He lifted the handle and pulled open the door.

I leaned forward to peer inside at the same time as Ms Walker. We nearly bumped heads.

We both saw the can of paint at the same time.

A small can of red paint resting on the locker floor.

The lid wasn't on tight. Splashes of red paint dripped over the side of the can.

"But it isn't *mine*!" Zeke wailed.

Ms Walker let out a long sigh. "I'm sorry, Zeke."

"It isn't mine!" Zeke whined. "Really, Ms Walker! It *isn't*!"

"I'm going to call your parents to come in for a serious talk," Ms Walker said, biting her lower lip. "And, of course, you're out of the play."

"Oh, nooo!" Zeke moaned. He slammed the locker door shut as hard as he could. The crash echoed down the long, empty hall.

Ms Walker flinched from the sound. She flashed Zeke an angry look. Then she turned to Brian and me. "So you two were also involved? Tell the truth!"

"No!" Brian and I both called out. "We didn't do it," I added. I started to say, "Neither did Zeke."

But I could see that it was too late. There was no way to argue against the can of paint in the locker.

Zeke was a cooked goose.

"If I find out that you and Brian had anything to do with it, I'll remove you from the play and call your parents in, too," Ms Walker threatened. "Now go home. All of you."

We turned and trudged out the door without another word.

The night air felt cold against my hot skin. I shivered.

The half-moon was covered by a sheet of grey

mist. The mist looked like a ghostly figure floating over the moon.

I followed Zeke and Brian down the concrete steps. A gust of wind made my jacket flap behind me.

"Do you believe it?" Zeke muttered angrily. "Do you believe it?"

"No," I replied, shaking my head. Poor Zeke. I could see he was really messed up. And when his parents got that call from Ms Walker, Zeke was going to be even *more* messed up!

"How did that paint get in your locker?" Brian asked him, his eyes peering into Zeke's.

Zeke turned away. "How should I know?" he snapped.

We made our way to the pavement. Zeke angrily kicked an empty cardboard juice carton into the street.

"See you tomorrow, I guess," Brian said unhappily. He gave us a little wave, then turned and started walking slowly towards his house.

Zeke jogged off in the other direction.

"Aren't you going to walk home with me?" I called.

"No," he shouted back, and kept going.

In a way I was glad he had left. I didn't really know what to say to him.

I just felt so bad.

I started walking slowly, my head down, thinking hard, when I saw a small, round light floating towards me through the darkness.

The light grew bigger. I realized it was a bicycle headlight. The bike turned out of the school car park and rolled smoothly, steadily towards me.

When it was a few feet away, I recognized the bike rider. "Tina!" I cried in surprise. "What are *you* doing here?"

She squealed to a stop, bouncing in the seat. Her dark eyes caught the light of the streetlamp above us. She smiled. An odd smile.

"Hi, Brooke. How's it going?" she asked.

Was she in the school? I wondered. Did she just come out of the school?"

"Where'd you come from?" I repeated.

Her strange smile remained on her face. "A friend's," she said. "I'm just coming from a friend's."

"Were you in the school?" I blurted out.

"The school? No. Not me," she replied. She shifted her weight, then raised her feet to the pedals. "Better zip up that jacket, Brooke," she said. "You don't want to catch a cold, do you?"

On Saturday we had play rehearsals all day long in the auditorium. The performance was only a week away.

We all worked hard, and the rehearsal went well. I only forgot my lines twice.

But it wasn't the same without Zeke.

Robert Hernandez had taken Zeke's place. I like Robert, but he's a very serious guy. He doesn't get my jokes, and he doesn't like to kid around or be kidded.

After lunch, Robert and Corey were rehearsing a scene together. Ms Walker still hadn't returned from lunch.

I wandered over to Brian. He had a paintbrush in his hand, dripping with black paint. He was leaning over the new backdrop, putting some final touches on the grey bricks.

"Looks good," I told him. I had a sudden urge to slap him on the back and make him smear black paint all over. But I decided that might not go over too well.

I don't know *where* these sudden urges come from.

"How's it going?" Brian asked without looking up. He was filling in some spots he had missed.

"Okay, I guess," I replied. Across the stage, I saw Tina working with a large glue pot. She was brushing a thick layer of glue on to a cardboard chandelier.

"Robert is going to be a good phantom," Brian said, scratching his chin with the tip of the paintbrush handle.

"Yeah," I agreed. "But I kind of miss Zeke."

Brian nodded. Then he turned to look up at me. "You know what? There hasn't been one practical joke since Zeke left. No scenery ruined. No mysterious phantoms leaping out at us. No threatening words scrawled on the walls. Nothing. Nothing bad since Ms Walker kicked Zeke out."

I hadn't thought about it until that second. But Brian was right. Ever since Zeke had been removed from the play, the Phantom had totally disappeared.

Everything had been going so smoothly. I hadn't even stopped to realize it.

Did this mean that Zeke actually was the Phantom? That Zeke had been doing all those horrible things after all?

"Did Zeke's parents have a cow when Ms Walker called them in to school?" Brian asked. "Did he get punished?"

"For sure," I replied, still thinking about the Phantom. "His parents grounded him for life. And they took away his VCR. That means no horror movies. Zeke can't *live* without horror movies!"

Brian sniggered. "Maybe Zeke has seen *too many* horror movies," he said.

"Okay, people!" a voice called loudly. I turned to see that Ms Walker had returned from lunch. "Let's take it from the opening of Act Two," she called. "We'll do the whole act."

I said goodbye to Brian and hurried to the front of the stage. Esmerelda was in just about every scene of Act Two. This time, I was determined to remember every word.

As I stepped beside Robert, I saw Ms Walker pick up her script from the table where she always left it. She grasped it in both hands and started to open it to Act Two.

I watched her expression change as her hands worked at the script. She let out a short, angry cry. Then she tugged some more at the thick script.

"Hey—" she shouted angrily. "Now who's the joker?"

"Ms Walker, what's wrong?" Robert called.

She raised the script and shook it furiously.

"The pages of my script—they've all been glued together!" she fumed.

Startled gasps rose up around the stage.

"That's *it*!" Ms Walker cried. She heaved the script at the wall. "That was the last joke! The play is cancelled! Everybody go home! It's cancelled!"

"Did Ms Walker change her mind?" Zeke asked.

I nodded. "Yeah. She calmed down after a few seconds and said the play could go on. But she was in a really bad mood for the rest of the day."

"At least this time she couldn't blame me," Zeke said quietly. He tossed a pink rubber ball across the living room, and Buster, his black cocker spaniel, went scrambling after it.

Brian and I had dropped by Zeke's house to tell him how things were going. Zeke was grounded—probably for ever—and couldn't leave the house. His parents were at the movies. They'd be home in a few hours.

Buster dropped the ball and started barking at Brian.

Zeke laughed. "He doesn't like you, Brian." He picked up the ball and bounced it over the carpet again.

But Buster ignored the ball and kept barking at Brian.

Brian blushed. He reached out to pet the dog's head. "What's your problem, fella? I'm not a bad guy."

Buster scampered away from Brian and crossed the room to search for the ball, which had rolled into the hallway.

"Well, I guess this proves there's some other joker in the class," Zeke said, his smile fading. He settled back on the couch. "Guess this proves that it wasn't me doing all the bad things."

I started to make a joke, but I caught the serious expression on Zeke's face. So I didn't say anything.

"There's a phantom, and it isn't me," Zeke said. "And now everyone thinks I'm a liar. Ms Walker thinks I tried to ruin the play. Even my parents think I've turned into a bad guy."

"You were a much better phantom than Robert," I said, trying to cheer him up. "There's less than a week to go, and Robert still keeps messing up his lines. He says he's sorry he auditioned for the play. He doesn't even want to be in it now."

Zeke jumped to his feet. "If we could prove that I'm not the Phantom, I'll bet Ms Walker would give the part back to me."

"Uh-oh," I said. I could see Zeke's mind working. I knew what he was going to say next.

"Uh-oh," Brian echoed. He also knew what Zeke was going to say.

"Let's go to school," Zeke said, his eyes wide with excitement. "Let's find the Phantom this time. I really want to get my part back."

I shook my head. "No way, Zeke—" I started.

"I really want to show everyone that I didn't try to ruin the play," Zeke insisted.

Brian tossed the ball to the dog. The dog watched it bounce away. "But you're grounded, remember?" Brian said to Zeke.

Zeke shrugged. "If we find the Phantom and prove that I'm innocent, my parents will be glad I went. And I won't be grounded any more. Come on, guys. One more try. Please?"

I stared back at Zeke, thinking hard. I didn't think it was a good idea. The last time we sneaked into the auditorium, we ended up in major trouble.

I could see by Brian's expression that he didn't want to go, either.

But how could we say no to Zeke? He was practically begging us!

It was a warm night, but I felt chilled just the same. As we walked to school, I kept seeing shadows moving close as if reaching for us. But when I turned to see them, they vanished.

Brooke, you have too much imagination, I scolded myself.

I wished my heart would stop thudding like a bass drum.

221

I wished I were home, watching TV with Jeremy. I had a bad feeling about our little adventure. A very bad feeling.

We didn't waste any time trying the doors. We climbed into the school through the same home economics room window. Then, once again we made our way silently down the dark halls to the auditorium.

One row of lights had been left on at the back of the seats. The stage lay dark and bare, except for the grey brick backdrop against the back wall.

Zeke led the way down the centre aisle. He had given us each a torch. We clicked them on as we made our way to the stage. The beams of light played over the empty rows of seats. I raised mine to the stage and swept it from side to side.

No one up there. No sign of anything unusual.

"Zeke, this is a waste of time," I said, whispering even though no one could hear us.

He raised a finger to his lips. "We're going down below the stage," Zeke said quietly, his eyes straight ahead. "And we're going to find him, Brooke. This time, we're going to find him."

I had never seen Zeke so serious, so determined. A chill of fear went slowly down my back. But I decided not to argue with him.

"Uh . . . maybe I should stay up on the stage while you two go down," Brian suggested. "I could stand guard."

222

"Stand guard against what?" Zeke demanded, raising his torch to Brian's face.

I could see Brian's frightened expression. "Against . . . anyone who might come," he replied weakly.

"All three of us have to go down," Zeke insisted. "If we do find the Phantom, I want two witnesses—you and Brooke."

"But the Phantom is a *ghost*—right?" Brian demanded. "How do we find a ghost?"

Zeke glared at him. "We'll find him."

Brian shrugged. We could both see that there was no point in arguing with Zeke tonight.

The floorboards on the stage creaked as we made our way to the trapdoor. Our torch moved over the outline of the square platform in the floor.

Brian and I huddled close together in the centre of the square. Zeke stomped hard on the little wooden peg, then jumped beside us.

We heard the familiar clanking sound. Then the gentle hum as the platform started to lower. The stage appeared to rise up all around us. In a few seconds, we were surrounded by four black walls.

The light from our torches washed over the walls as we sank lower and lower under the stage. My heart felt as if it were sinking, too—down to my knees!

The three of us stood pressed together in the

223

centre of the platform. The clanking and grinding sounds grew louder as we went down. Finally, we hit the bottom with a hard *thud*.

For a few seconds, none of us moved.

Zeke was the first to step off the platform. He raised his torch and swept it slowly around. We were in the middle of a large, empty chamber. It tunnelled out in two directions.

"Here, Phantom! Here, boy!" Zeke called softly, as if calling his dog. "Here, Phantom. Where *are* you, Phantom?" he called in a singsong voice.

I stepped off the platform and gave him a shove. "Stop it," I insisted. "I thought you were serious about this. Why are you making a joke of it?"

"Just trying to keep you from getting too scared," Zeke replied. But, of course, I knew the truth. He was trying to keep *himself* from getting too scared.

I turned back to Brian. In the dim light, he looked scared enough for both of us! "There's no one down here. Can we go back up now?" he pleaded.

"No way," Zeke told him. "Follow me. Keep your light down on the ground so we can see where we're going."

Walking side by side, Brian and I followed Zeke into the chamber. We stepped into a long tunnel, took a few steps, then stopped to listen.

Silence.

My legs were trembling. In fact, my entire body was shaking. But Zeke was acting so brave. There was no way I'd let him know how frightened I was.

"This tunnel probably stretches all the way under the school," Zeke whispered, moving his light ahead of us. "Maybe even farther. Maybe it goes under the entire block!"

We took another few steps—then stopped when we heard a noise behind us.

A clanking, followed by a loud hum.

"Hey!" Brian cried out shrilly. "The trap-door!"

All three of us spun around and started running back towards it. Our heavy footsteps echoed loudly through the dark tunnel.

My chest was aching so hard by the time we got back to the trapdoor platform, I could hardly breathe.

"It—it's going back up!" Zeke cried.

We stood there helplessly, gazing at the platform as it rose over our heads, climbing back up to the stage.

"Push the switch!" Zeke cried to me. "Bring it back down!"

I fumbled on the wall till I found the switch. I tried to move it. But it was stuck.

No. It had been locked.

It wouldn't budge.

The trapdoor platform stood high above us. A heavy silence fell over the three of us as we stared up in the darkness.

"Zeke, now we're trapped down here," I uttered. "There's no way back up. We're totally trapped."

We waited to see if someone was coming down. But the trapdoor remained closed up there.

Brian let out a frightened sigh. "Somebody did it," he whispered, staring up to the platform. "Somebody pushed the switch and sent it back up."

"The Phantom!" I cried. I turned to Zeke. "Now what?"

Zeke shrugged. "Now we have no choice. If we want to get *out* of here, we *have* to find the Phantom!"

Our circles of yellow light trembled over the floor as we turned and headed back into the tunnel. No one said a word as we followed it around one curve, then another.

The floor became soft and muddy. The air grew cooler.

I heard a soft, chittering sound in the distance. I hoped it wasn't a bat.

Brian and I had to hurry to keep up with Zeke.

He was taking long strides, his torch swinging back and forth in front of him.

Suddenly, I heard low, musical humming. It took me a while to realize it was coming from Zeke. He was humming a tune to himself.

Come on, Zeke, give me a break! I thought. You've *got* to be scared! You can't fool me with a little cheerful humming. You are as scared as I am!

I started to tease him about it. But the tunnel suddenly ended, and we found ourselves at a low doorway. Brian hung back. But Zeke and I stepped up to the door, our torches beaming over it.

"Anyone in there?" Zeke called in a strange, tiny voice.

No reply.

I reached out and pushed the door. It creaked open. Zeke and I raised our torches and aimed them inside.

A room. Fully furnished. I saw a folding chair. A beat-up couch with one of the cushions missing. Bookshelves along one wall.

My torch fell over a small table. A bowl and a box of cornflakes stood on the table. I swept the light around and saw a small, unmade bed against the far wall.

Zeke and Brian followed me into the room. Our beams of light slid slowly over every object, every piece of furniture. An old-fashioned record player stood on a low table. A stack of old records was piled beside it.

"Do you *believe* this?" Zeke whispered. A grin spread over his face.

"I think we've found the Phantom's home," I whispered back.

His torch tilting in front of him, Brian made his way to the table. He peered down at the cereal bowl. "The Phantom—he was just there," Brian said. "The cereal isn't soggy yet."

"This is amazing!" I cried. "Someone actually lives down here, way below the—"

I stopped because I felt a sneeze coming on. Maybe a whole sneezing fit.

I tried to hold it in. But I couldn't. I sneezed once. Twice. Five times.

"Stop it, Brooke!" Brian pleaded. "He'll *hear* you!"

"But we *want* to find him," Zeke reminded Brian.

I sneezed seven times. Then one more for good luck. Finally, I was all sneezed out.

"He heard that. I *know* he did," Brian fretted. His eyes darted around in fear.

The door slammed shut.

"Nooo!" We all jumped and cried out.

My heart leaped to my mouth. Every muscle in my body tied itself into a knot.

We turned to stare at the door. Someone had

closed it, I knew. It hadn't been blown shut by any wind.

Zeke was the first to move. Lowering his torch, he hurtled to the door. He grabbed the knob and pushed hard.

The door didn't budge.

Zeke lowered his shoulder against the door. Twisting the knob, he pushed again.

Still no success.

He banged his shoulder against the door. Pushed again. Strained against the door with all his weight.

When he turned back to us, his face revealed his fear for the first time. "We—we're locked in," he said softly.

I rushed up beside Zeke. "Maybe if all three of us try," I suggested.

"Maybe," Zeke replied. But I could see he didn't have much hope.

I swallowed hard. Seeing Zeke so frightened made me even *more* frightened.

"Yeah. Let's all push together," Brian agreed, stepping up beside me. "We can *break* the door down if we have to."

Way to go, Brian! I thought. He's finally showing some spirit.

We lined up against the door and prepared to push.

I took another deep breath and held it. I was trying to calm myself down. My arms and legs felt as if they were made of chewing gum.

This is just so scary, I realized. If we are locked in this tiny room and can't get out, we could be here for the rest of our lives. We are miles and miles away from the rest of the world.

Everyone will search and search up above. And they'll never find us. And even if we yell and scream at the tops of our lungs for help, there's no way anyone could hear us.

We'll be trapped here for ever.

I took another deep breath. "Okay, on the count of three," I said. "On three, everybody push."

Zeke started to count. "One . . . two . . ."

"Whoa! Wait a minute!" I interrupted. I stared at the door. "We pushed the door to get in here—right?"

"Yeah, I guess," Zeke replied, staring hard at me.

"So it won't *push* open from inside," I said. "We have to *pull* it open."

"Hey—you're right!" Zeke cried.

I grabbed the knob, twisted it, and pulled hard. The door slid open easily.

And there was a man standing in the doorway.

My torch moved up to his face. I recognized him instantly.

Emile. The little, white-haired man who said he was the night janitor.

He blocked the doorway and glared in at us, an ugly, menacing scowl on his scarred face.

"Let us go!" I shrieked.

He didn't move. His strange, grey eyes moved from Zeke to Brian to me.

"You have to let us out of here!" I insisted. And then I added meekly, "Please?"

His scowl grew even angrier. The light from the torch made the long scar on his cheek look even deeper.

He didn't budge from the doorway. "Why are you down here?" he demanded in his hoarse whisper of a voice. "Why are you in my home?"

"So—you *are* the Phantom!" I blurted out.

He narrowed his eyes at me in surprise. "Phantom?" His expression turned thoughtful. "I guess you could call me that."

Brian uttered a low cry.

"This is my home sweet home," the man said angrily. "Why are you here? Why didn't you listen to my warnings?"

"Your warnings?" I asked. I was shaking so

233

hard, the light from my torch was dancing all over the wall.

"I did everything I could to keep you away," the Phantom said. "To keep you from my home."

"You mean the paint on the backdrop? Swinging down from the catwalk? The scary mask in my locker with the note?" I cried in astonishment.

The Phantom nodded. "I tried to warn you. I didn't want to hurt anyone. But I had to protect my home."

"And so you tried to stop our play?" Zeke demanded, huddling close to me. "You tried to ruin our play so we wouldn't use the trapdoor and find you down here?"

The Phantom nodded.

"And what happened seventy-two years ago?" I asked him. "What happened to you the first time the play was supposed to be performed? Why did you disappear that night?"

The Phantom's expression changed. I saw confusion in his silvery eyes. "I—I don't understand," he stammered, staring hard at me, his white hair falling over his forehead.

"Seventy-two years ago," I insisted.

A bitter smile formed on his lips. "Hey, I'm not *that* old!" he replied. "I'm only fifty-seven."

"Then . . . you're not the Phantom?" Zeke asked uncertainly.

Emile shook his head. He let out a weary sigh.

"I don't understand this Phantom talk, young man. I'm just a poor homeless guy trying to protect my little space."

All three of us studied him, trying to decide if he was telling the truth. I decided that he was. "You've been living here under the school?" I asked softly. "How did you know about this room down here?"

"My father worked at the school for thirty years," Emile replied. "He used to bring me here with him when I was a kid. When I lost my apartment in town, I remembered this space. I've been living here ever since. For nearly six months now."

His eyes glared angrily again. He brushed the hair off his forehead as his ugly scowl returned. "But you're ruining it for me, aren't you?" he said sharply. "You're ruining it all for me."

He moved quickly, stepping from the doorway, entering the room, walking towards us with that menacing expression.

I stumbled back. "Wh-what are you going to do to us?" I cried.

"You've ruined everything. Everything," he repeated, moving towards us.

"Now, wait—" I cried, raising my hands as if to shield myself.

Then I heard a sound. From out in the tunnel. A low clanking sound.

I turned to Zeke and Brian. They heard it, too.

The trapdoor! It was moving. Coming down. We could hear it at the other end of the tunnel.

I think all three of us had the same idea at once. We *had* to get to that trapdoor. It was our only chance of escape.

"You've ruined everything," Emile repeated, suddenly sounding more sad than angry. "Why didn't you listen to my warnings?"

Without saying a word to each other, Zeke, Brian and I charged for the door. "Oh!" I bumped into Emile as I scooted past.

To my surprise, he didn't reach out to grab me, didn't try to stop me.

I led the way out of the door, running at full speed. My legs still felt as rubbery as chewing gum. But I forced them to move. One running step, then another.

I didn't glance back. But I could hear Zeke and Brian at my heels. And then I heard Emile's voice echoing through the tunnels: "You've ruined everything. Everything!"

Was Emile chasing after us?

I didn't care. I just wanted to get to that trapdoor platform and get out of there!

I plunged blindly through the dark, curving tunnel. My trainers sank into the soft dirt floor as I ran. My shoulder scraped the rough wall, but I didn't slow down.

The light bounced over the ground at my feet. I raised it as the trapdoor platform came into view. I was gasping for breath. My side ached from running.

"Huh? What are *you* doing down here?" a man's voice called.

Zeke's dad!

Zeke, Brian and I scrambled on to the platform, squeezing beside him.

"What's going on?" Mr Matthews demanded. "Whose voice is that?"

"Up!" I managed to choke out. "Take us up."

Zeke reached out and flipped the switch. This time it moved.

With a hard jerk, the platform started to raise itself.

I gazed back to the tunnel. Had Emile followed after us?

No. No sign of him.

He hadn't even chased us.

Weird, I thought. So weird.

"I heard a man's voice. Who was that?" Mr Matthews demanded again.

"A homeless guy. Living beneath the stage," I said, explaining what happened and how he had been trying to scare us for weeks.

"How did you know we were down there?" Zeke asked his dad.

"You were supposed to be at home," he replied sternly. "You were grounded. You're *still* grounded. But when you weren't at home, I figured I'd find you poking around the stage again. The side door to the school was open. I entered the auditorium and heard the trap-door moving. I decided to see what was going on."

"I'm so glad!" I cried. I felt like hugging Mr Matthews.

As soon as the platform stopped, we scrambled to the stage. Zeke's dad hurried to call the police. He told them there was a homeless guy living under the school.

The police arrived quickly. We watched them go down the trapdoor. We waited for them to bring Emile up. But they returned a few minutes later without him.

"No one down there," an officer reported. He removed his helmet and scratched his black, wavy hair. "No sign of anyone, either. Just a bed and some old furniture."

"What about his food? His books?" I asked.

"All gone," the officer replied. "Guess he cleared out real fast. The basement door was still slightly open.

After the police left, Brian said good night and headed out of the auditorium. Zeke's dad was going to drive me home.

I turned to Zeke. "So, there's your Phantom," I said with a little sadness. "Just a poor homeless man. Not a seventy-two-year-old ghost who's been haunting the school since it was built. Just a poor homeless man."

"Yeah, it's disappointing," Zeke replied, frowning. "I really wanted to meet a real ghost, a real phantom." His expression brightened. "But at least now Ms Walker will believe me. And I'll get my part in the play back."

The play. I'd almost forgotten about the play.

Zeke was right, I thought happily. He'll get his part back now. Everything will go fine.

The Phantom is gone.

Now we can all relax, I thought. Now we can enjoy ourselves and put on a great peformance.

Wow. Was I wrong!

24

The night of the performance, I sat in the girls' dressing room, smearing globs of stage make-up all over my face. I'd never worn so much make-up before, and didn't think I was doing it right. I didn't even want to wear the gunk in the first place.

But Ms Walker said we all had to. Even the guys. She said it cuts down on the glare from the lights and makes your face less shiny on-stage.

It was a wild scene in the girls' dressing room. We were all struggling into our costumes and brushing on make-up. Lisa Rego and Gia Bentley—two fifth-graders who didn't even have big parts in the play—were hogging the full-length mirror, laughing and giggling and admiring themselves.

By the time I got to check myself out, the stage manager was calling, "Places! Places, everyone!"

My stomach jumped. Calm down, Brooke, I

ordered myself. This is supposed to be fun—
remember?

I stepped out of the dressing room, crossed the
hall, entered the auditorium through the stage
door, and took my place at the side of the stage.
Someone tapped me on the shoulder, and I
jumped a mile. Man, was I jittery!

I whirled around and found myself face-to-
face with the Phantom!

I knew it was only Zeke in his costume and
mask, but he startled me just the same. "Zeke!
You look so *real*! You look awesome!" I told him.

Zeke didn't reply. He gave me a very formal
bow from the waist, then hurried to take his
place.

The curtain was closed. But I could hear the
steady rumble of voices out in the auditorium. I
peeked out of the side of the curtain. Wow! Every
seat was filled. That thought sent my stomach
doing jumping jacks all over again.

The lights began to dim. The audience instantly became silent. The stage lights went up.
The music started.

Go for it, Brooke, I told myself. Just go for it!

The play didn't get strange until the end of
the first act. We were all doing really well until
then.

When the curtain opened, and the audience
applauded the set, I stepped out on-stage with

241

Corey. And I completely forgot about my stage fright.

"Be careful, daughter," Corey warned, playing my father. "There's a creature living beneath this theatre. A twisted phantom, scarred and ugly."

"I do not believe you, Father," I replied as Esmerelda. "You are only trying to control me, to keep me a child!"

The audience seemed to be having a great time. They laughed in the right places and applauded several times.

This is *excellent*! I thought. I was excited without being nervous. I was enjoying every minute of the performance.

And as the first act drew near its end, I knew the real highlight of the show was coming. A fog of dry ice swept slowly over the stage. Blue lights swirled through the twisting fog, making it appear eerie and unreal.

I heard the clank of the trapdoor. I knew it was carrying Zeke in his Phantom costume up from down below.

In seconds, the Phantom would make his big entrance, rising up in the blue fog.

The audience will love it, I thought, watching the fog billow up over my long, yellow dress.

"Phantom, is that you?" I called. "Are you coming to see me?"

The Phantom's blue-and-green mask floated

up in the fog. Then his black-caped shoulders hovered into view.

The audience gasped and then cheered as the Phantom rose, standing stiffly in the fog, his black cape billowing out behind him.

And then he stepped towards me, walking slowly, majestically.

"Oh, Phantom! We are together at last!" I cried with all the emotion I could put into it. "I have dreamed of this moment for so long!"

I took his gloved hand and led him through the swirls of blue fog to the front of the stage.

A white spotlight captured us both.

I turned to face him. Stared into his eyes behind the blue-and-green mask.

And realized instantly that it wasn't Zeke!

I started to cry out. But he squeezed my hand.

His eyes burned into mine. He seemed to be begging me with his eyes, begging me not to say anything, not to give him away.

Who *is* he? I wondered, frozen in the bright spotlight. Why does he look familiar?

I turned back to the audience. Silent. Waiting for me to speak.

I took a deep breath and said Esmerelda's next line. "Phantom, why do you haunt this theatre? Please tell me your story. I will not be afraid."

The Phantom swept his cape behind him. His eyes were still locked on mine. His gloved hand still squeezed mine tightly, as if to keep me from escaping.

"I have lived under this theatre for more than seventy years," he declared. "My story is a sad one. You might even call it tragic, my fair Esmerelda."

"Please continue!" I exclaimed.

Who is he? I asked myself. *Who?*

"I was chosen to star in a play," the Phantom revealed. "A play in this very theatre. It was to be the greatest night of my life!"

He paused to take a long, deep breath.

My heart skipped a beat. He isn't reciting the script, I realized. Those aren't the right words.

What is he saying?

"But my great night was never to be!" the Phantom continued, still gripping my hand. "You see, my dear Esmerelda, an hour before the play was to begin, I fell. I plunged to my death!"

I gasped. He was pointing to the trapdoor.

I realized who he was now. He was the boy who had disappeared. The boy, seventy-two years ago, who was to star as the Phantom. But disappeared and was never found.

Here he was, standing beside me on the same stage. Here he was, revealing to us all how he had disappeared, why the play was never performed.

"There!" he cried, pointing to the opening in the stage floor. "That's where I fell! There! I fell to my death. I became a real phantom. And I've waited down there ever since, waiting, waiting. Hoping for a night like tonight where I could finally play my greatest role!"

As he finished this speech, the audience burst into cheers and loud applause.

They think it's part of the play, I realized.

They don't know the true pain behind his words. They don't know that he's revealing his true story to them.

The Phantom took a deep bow. The applause grew even louder.

The fog billowed over us both.

Who is he? Who?

The question repeated in my mind.

I had to know the answer. I had to know who the Phantom was.

As he stood up from his bow, I pulled my hand free of his.

Then I reached up—and tugged off his mask!

I squinted into the thick, blue fog, desperate to see his face.

The bright spotlight flashed in my eyes, blinding me for a moment.

In that moment, the Phantom covered his face with both hands.

I reached to pull away his hands.

"No!" he screamed. "No—you can't!"

He staggered back, away from me.

Staggered and lost his balance.

"No! No!" he cried. "You can't! You can't!"

And toppled backwards.

Into the open trapdoor.

And vanished in the swirling blue fog.

I heard his scream all the way down.

Then silence.

A horrible, still silence.

The audience rose to its feet and burst into loud applause and cries of "Bravo!"

They all thought it was part of the play.

247

But I knew better. I knew that the Phantom had finally revealed himself after seventy-two years. That he had finally had his moment on the stage.

And that he had died all over again.

As the curtain closed, muffling the excited cheers of the audience, I stood at the opening in the floor, my hands pressed to my face.

I couldn't speak. I couldn't move.

I stared down into the hole in the floor and saw only blackness.

Then, raising my eyes, I saw Zeke running across the stage to me. Wearing jeans and a white T-shirt, he lurched towards me, his expression dazed.

"Zeke!" I cried.

"Ow. Someone hit me, I think," he moaned, rubbing the back of his head. "I've been out cold." He raised his eyes to mine. "Brooke, are you okay? Did—?"

"The Phantom!" I cried. "He took your part, Zeke. He—he's down there!" I pointed into the opening. "We've got to find him!"

I stepped on the peg. The trapdoor clanked and groaned. The platform returned to the top.

Zeke and I climbed aboard.

We rode it down, down to the dark chamber below.

We searched every corner. We didn't find him.

We didn't find the mask. Or the costume. Or anything.

Somehow I knew we wouldn't.

Somehow I knew we would never see him again.

"Great job, people! Great job!" Ms Walker called to us as we trooped off-stage. "Phantom, I liked the new lines you added! Great job! See you all at the cast party!"

Zeke and I struggled to get to the dressing room so we could get changed. But we were mobbed by people who wanted to congratulate us and tell us how talented and terrific we were.

The play was a major success!

I searched for Brian. I wanted to tell him all about the Phantom. But I couldn't see him in the excited crowd of friends and parents.

"Come on—let's get out of here!" Zeke cried. He pulled me by the hand out of the auditorium and into the hall.

"Wow! We're a hit!" I exclaimed, feeling totally wrecked and pumped and dazed and crazed, all at the same time.

"Let's just get our coats and get changed at home," Zeke suggested. "We can try to figure out who played my part on the way. Then we can meet at my house to go to the party."

"Okay," I agreed. "But we have to hurry. My

parents are waiting to tell me what a fabulous star I am!"

The sound of excited chattering and laughter drifted from the auditorium and followed us as we made our way to our lockers.

"Hey—" I stopped in front of my locker. "Look, Zeke—the door is open. I didn't leave it unlocked."

"Weird," Zeke murmured.

I pulled the door all the way open, and a book toppled out on to the floor.

I bent to pick it up. It was an old book, its brown cover worn and dusty. I turned it around, squinting to read the cover in the dim hall light.

"It's a really old yearbook," I told Zeke. "Look. It's from this school. Woods Mill. But it's from the 1920s."

"Huh? How'd it get in your locker?" Zeke asked, staring down at it.

My eyes fell on a torn sheet of paper tucked inside. A bookmark.

Gripping the heavy, old book in both hands, I opened to the pages marked by the bookmark.

"Wow!" Zeke cried. "I don't believe it!"

We were staring at a yearbook article about the play we had just performed. "*The Phantom* To Be Performed in the Spring," read the headline at the top.

"This must have been written early that school year," I said. "We know the play was never performed. We know the whole story of what happened back then."

"Hold the book up to the light," Zeke instructed. "Let's check out the pictures."

I raised the book, and we both stared down at the small photographs that covered the two pages.

Then we saw it.

A small, blurred black-and-white photo of the boy who had won the starring role, the boy who was to play the Phantom. The boy who had disappeared.

The boy was Brian.